T0165202

Silver Moon

The Legend of the Wolf People

Silver Moon

The Legend of the Wolf People

Wayde Bulow

iUniverse, Inc.
New York Bloomington

Silver Moon
The Legend of the Wolf People

Copyright © 2009 by Wayde Bulow

*All rights reserved. No part of this book may be used or reproduced by any means,
graphic, electronic, or mechanical, including photocopying, recording, taping or by any
information storage retrieval system without the written permission of the publisher
except in the case of brief quotations embodied in critical articles and reviews.*

*This is a work of fiction. All of the characters, names, incidents, organizations, and dialogue
in this novel are either the products of the author's imagination or are used fictitiously.*

iUniverse books may be ordered through booksellers or by contacting:

*iUniverse
1663 Liberty Drive
Bloomington, IN 47403
www.iuniverse.com
1-800-Authors (1-800-288-4677)*

*Because of the dynamic nature of the Internet, any Web addresses or links contained in this book
may have changed since publication and may no longer be valid. The views expressed in this work
are solely those of the author and do not necessarily reflect the views of the publisher, and the
publisher hereby disclaims any responsibility for them.*

ISBN: 978-1-4401-4426-4 (pbk)
ISBN: 978-1-4401-4427-1 (ebk)

Printed in the United States of America

iUniverse rev. date: 5/21/2009

For my family.

Contents

Introduction

Running Bear said the wolf people live in the far mountains to the north where no Indian will go. When the moon is full they turn into the demon monsters of legend. Chato was more powerful than any of his people before him. Turning into the wolf at will, he was not affected by the full moon. With the promise of beaver and mining opportunities the outside world poured into the wolves' domain. Soon bloodshed and terror spread over the mountain like a wildfire with the deaths of the invaders fueling the flames. Once the wolves were loose, what would their future be as they spread their curse upon the world below.

Legend of the Wolf

An eagle soared effortlessly on gentle wind currents rising above the mountainside. The tips of its outstretched wings caressed the wind like a painter's brush stroking a canvas. Tall, green pine trees reached upward into the eagle's domain. Hide-covered tepees dotted the valley floor, surrounded by lush meadow grass. A mountain stream wound its way down the valley like a snake, carrying its cold blue water into the plains beyond.

A young man dressed in dark tan buckskins and wearing a hat made from a skunk pelt watched the eagle soaring high above. He wished he could see the world from the eagle's eyes and travel with the wind wherever he wanted to go. He watched as the eagle rode the wind farther and farther away, until it was only a small spot above the mountaintops.

"Jack," a stern voice said.

"Jack!" it yelled again, getting more upset.

Jack turned from the disappearing eagle and looked quickly at the man sitting at his side. "Yes, Reverend Gipson, what is it?"

Reverend Gipson was a tall man dressed in a soft buckskin hunting shirt and fringed jacket stained dark by the smoke of many campfires. He wore homespun pants tucked into tall leather moccasins. A hat made from a wolf pelt was pressed firmly down on his head, its heavy leather bill shielding his green eyes from the sun. Long, black hair hung down over his shoulders, partially covered by the wolf skin. His beard hung down his chest, and his eyes were hidden in his face by his beard and long, beak-like nose.

"Get the rest of the trade goods from the packhorse!" he told Jack in a gruff voice.

Jack got up and walked carefully back to the packhorse, surrounded by Indian women and children. Removing a heavy leather bag from the packsaddle, he sat it on the ground and opened it. It was filled with glass beads and trinkets of every size and shape. Reaching his hand into the bag, he searched for something he had seen earlier. It was a silver wolf emblem on a silver chain and was much too nice a gift to be given away to these Indians. Quickly he put it into a leather possibles bag hanging on his belt. Closing the bag full of trinkets, he took it to the reverend. Opening the bag, the reverend poured most of the contents out on a buffalo robe. The women and children's eyes all grew large as they looked down at the treasures spread out before them. The chief of the village sat cross-legged across from Reverend Gibson, surrounded by his warriors. An old man, the chief's gray braids hung down his chest, wrapped tightly in soft leather and fur. Three large eagle feathers were tied to the hair on the back of his head and stood straight up like an outstretched hand. His face was wrinkled and old, but his black eyes were fiery and watched everything.

"I bring these gifts to Running Bear and his people," the reverend said, pointing at the treasures scattered on the robe.

"What is it the white man wants?" Running Bear asked in a deep voice.

"I wish to learn more about your neighbors to the north, the wolf people," the reverend replied. Running Bear looked surprised. The women and children gasped and backed up several steps.

Regaining his composure, Running Bear looked deep into the reverend's eyes and asked, "Why you want to know about the people to the north?"

"I have never traded with these people and would like to."

"You must stay away from their country if you value your life," Running Bear told him. "From my grandfather's, grandfather's time, we have never gone into their country. Legends tell of fierce warriors who attack with arrows and clubs during the day and return at night as demon wolves to eat both the dead and the living." The chief was clearly shaken just talking about the wolf tribe.

"It is said that the wolf tribe's country is filled with mountain streams, harboring many beavers," the reverend said in a matter-of-fact voice.

"I do not know," the old chief stated. "My people have never gone into their country."

"In one moon I plan to lead an expedition of company trappers into their country to trap for the season," Reverend Gipson said.

"Then I say goodbye to you now, for you will never return!"

"Is there a way to fight the demon wolves?" Reverend Gipson asked the chief. Running Bear looked deep into the reverend's eyes and then said something to a warrior at his side who turned and quickly left.

"It is said," Running Bear replied, clearing the fear from his throat, "that the only way to kill the wolf people is with arrows tipped with the sacred stone." The returning warrior rushed to his side and handed the chief a stone the size of a man's head. "If the shiny rock pierces the wolf warrior's heart, he will die forever." Handing the rock to Reverend Gipson, he watched as Jack and the reverend examined the stone.

"It's silver," Jack told the reverend the minute he saw the vein of shiny ore in the black rock.

"Are you sure?" asked the reverend.

"Yes, I worked in a silver mine before I came west to trap," Jack told him.

"When the moon is full you can hear the eerie howls of the wolf demons late at night," Running Bear told them.

"Are you sure they aren't just the howls of timber wolves running in a pack?" Reverend Gipson asked.

Angered by the white man's doubt, Running Bear's face grew stern and his dark eyes glowed. "White man, you will know when you hear the demon wolf howl, because the hair on the back of your neck will stand up and your skin will tingle with fear! Legends speak of a cave high upon their mountain where the demon wolves gather and feast on the dead!" Running Bear said loudly, frightening all the women and children standing around him.

Reverend Gipson looked quickly at Jack and told him quietly it was time for them to go before the old chief got any madder. "Take these gifts, my friend, for the wise words you have spoken about the wolf people," the reverend said as he and Jack stood up. "In one moon I will journey into their country to trap and trade. When I return I will visit you and your people and tell you what I've learned." Waving goodbye, the reverend and Jack mounted their ponies and rode out of the village, leading the packhorse. Running Bear watched them ride away and knew he would never see the foolish white men again. Smiling to himself, he hoped the company trappers would be enough raw meat to keep the wolf people content in their country and not venture into his.

Jack and the reverend rode hard the rest of the day down the mountain and away from the Indian village. All the way down the mountain Jack thought about what the old chief had told them. *Silver in their heart will kill them*, he thought as he toyed with the silver wolf emblem on a chain in his possibles bag. He looked at the silver trinket. He would much rather win some Indian maiden's heart with his beautiful wolf emblem than cast it into a silver ball to kill imaginary wolf demons. He laughed to himself as he rode down the mountain thinking of how scared the chief and his people looked when Reverend Gipson first mentioned the wolf people. He was glad they were going into the wolf tribe's country. If he were lucky, he would catch more beaver than anyone and be rich before his twentieth birthday, only ten months away. When he became rich, he would steal the heart of a beautiful Indian princess, take her away to trap and raise a family.

That night they camped in the foothills of the mountains on a hillside covered in aspen trees and surrounded by pines. Jack built a fire pit and soon had a good fire going, while the reverend tended their horses. Reverend Gipson hadn't said anything since they left the Indian village. He stood with the rifle in the crook of his arm, watching the surrounding foothills in the last rays of daylight. As darkness crept across the mountainside, Jack walked up to the fire carrying a load of firewood.

"Reverend, you don't believe what Running Bear told us do you?" Jack asked.

"Running Bear is a great chief and a brave warrior, and his lodge is full of enemy scalps. I'm not sure what to believe when I see a warrior of his magnitude get rattled by just mentioning the wolf people," Reverend Gipson told Jack in a puzzled voice.

"Maybe he is just getting old," Jack replied.

"Maybe," the reverend said, filling his pipe full of tobacco and lighting it. Jack put coffee on to brew and passed out several sticks of thick jerky for their supper. It was pitch-black away from the fire with no moon and very few stars in the cloudy sky. Sitting next to the warmth of the fire, Jack started to get sleepy. His eyelids became heavier and heavier until they closed. Suddenly, a piercing wolf howl broke the silence of the darkness. Jack jumped up, wide awake, and threw his coffee cup high into the air. He saw Reverend Gipson raise his rifle. Jack lunged for his own rifle and sat there, ready for whatever was to come. They were both tense, rifles cocked, as they tried desperately to see in the darkness.

"I guess it was just a wolf," the reverend said in a quiet voice as he un-cocked his rifle.

"Yeah, I guess so," Jack replied as he lowered the hammer on his rifle.

"It was only a wolf," the reverend said, smiling. "My skin doesn't tingle with fear, but the hairs on the back of my neck did stand up."

They both enjoyed a good laugh, trying to convince each other it wasn't a demon.

"Well, it's time to bring the horses in for the night," the reverend said as he stood. Following him into the darkness, Jack quickly caught his horse and the packhorse. Removing their hobbles, he led them back to camp and tied them up. He could hear aspen leaves gently rattling in the soft wind. After returning to the fire, Jack saw the reverend had already turned in. He looked at the reverend lying still under his blanket and knew he was lucky to have found a friend like Reverend Gipson. He wasn't really a reverend, or at least Jack didn't think he was. He commanded a bunch of company trappers over thirty strong. He had taken Jack under his wing and was like the older brother Jack never had. As Jack curled up next to the fire, rifle close by, he closed his eyes and tried to sleep. The minute he closed his eyes he saw Running Bear warning them not to enter the wolf tribe's country. He dreamt of demon wolf warriors, fangs dripping saliva, chasing him through the forest. As he tossed and turned, fleeing for his life, he saw a vicious wolf turn into a beautiful Indian maiden with large fawn eyes and long flowing hair. She reached her small hand out to him, beckoning him to her when suddenly she turned back into a wolf demon and sank her fangs deep into his arm. Screaming, he woke to find the reverend bending over him, shaking his shoulder.

"Take it easy," said the reverend. "I just wanted to wake you—it's time to move on." Jack stared wide-eyed at the reverend in disbelief for a few seconds before sitting up.

"I just had a terrible dream!" he told Reverend Gibson.

"You must have from the way you jumped and screamed when I woke you." Quickly they broke camp and saddled up, riding out as the sun peeked over the mountaintops. Early that afternoon they rode over a tall sagebrush-covered ridge and down into a river valley. At the top of the ridge they waved to a sentry, posted there to watch for danger.

"Are we pulling out to trap tomorrow, Reverend?" the sentry asked as they rode past.

Turning in his saddle the reverend replied, "As soon as our hunting parties have brought in enough game to last the winter, we will start trapping." Once they arrived at camp, the company trappers were glad to see that the reverend and Jack had return. They were eager to find out what they had learned. That night around the campfire, Reverend Gibson told them what chief Running Bear had said.

"Did he say the streams were full of beaver?" one trapper asked.

"He said he never knew, because they never went there," the reverend answered.

"I'll bet he's lying," another trapper growled. "He knows there are beaver all over that mountain but doesn't want us to trap them."

"I don't know for sure, but one thing I do know is Running Bear and his people are deathly afraid of the wolf people," the reverend replied.

"Men who turn into wolves and eat people, smells like rotten meat to me!" another trapper yelled out as everyone nodded in agreement.

"I've never had any problem killing wolves before, so I don't spect to start having troubles now!" a huge trapper snarled, drawing his knife and pretending to slit his own throat.

"All I want to know is when do we start catching all those beaver?" a trapper yelled to Reverend Gipson.

"As soon as we have enough dried meat to last us through the winter," the reverend replied.

"Our hunting parties have been bringing game in daily," the big trapper told him. "In a couple more weeks we should be ready."

"That's what I figured also," the reverend told the others. "The sooner we get supplied with meat, the sooner we can get started." Everyone cheered and said they would step up the hunting at sunrise in order to keep the drying racks full of meat.

For two weeks the trappers labored, tending the drying fires and butchering fresh game. Reverend Gibson was still bothered with Running Bear's warnings about the wolf people. In secret, when no one was watching, he melted down several silver coins and trinkets. When he was done, he had three fifty-caliber rifle balls. He wanted to cast more balls from silver but couldn't find any more silver trinkets. He remembered a silver wolf pendant on a chain he had seen in the trade goods, but he was sure they had given it to Running Bear's people before they left the village. It was a shame because he could have cast at least one more musket ball from it. He also had another trick up his sleeve if the wolf people were as bad as Running Bear said. He had several kegs of gunpowder he could use to blast shut any cave opening they might find. He was sure he was overreacting, but still, one never knew.

Wolf Mountain

Everyone was excited as they loaded up all their supplies and headed for the wolf tribe's country. They had been getting ready for several days now and it was all Reverend Gipson could do to keep them focused. Jack spent all of his time at the river camp drying meat and hoping he would never see another drying rack for a long time. *Still,* he thought to himself as he chewed on a piece of jerky and rode away from the camp, *the meat tasted good.* Following a long line of trappers, he wondered what kind of horrors they would find in the far mountains where the wolf people lived. He looked at his arm where the demon wolf had bit him in his dream. It was so real he had to pull up his leather sleeve to make sure there were no bite marks. Feeling foolish, he quickly pulled his sleeve down before someone saw him. He could still see the Indian maiden with her beautiful fawn eyes and raven black hair looking dainty and helpless turn into a demon wolf with yellow eyes and huge teeth. Even now the image of the demon wolf frightened him, and he could feel goose bumps up and down his arms.

"Hey Jack, are you all right?" a trapper in front of him asked, leaning back in his saddle. Snapping out of his daydream, Jack blushed and said he was fine, almost choking on a mouthful of jerky.

For two days they traveled towards the wolf people's country. On the afternoon of the third day, the mountain loomed high above them. It was almost dark when Reverend Gipson called a halt. He told the trappers they would wait until morning before they invaded the wolf tribe's mountains. Jack helped tend the horses with the other trappers and then returned to the cooking fires, looking for something to eat.

Filling a wooden bowl full of tasty stew, he was just getting started wolfing down the food when Reverend Gibson found him.

"Jack, when we ride into the wolf tribe's country tomorrow, I want you to stay close by me. I don't know what kind of trouble we might run into, but at least with you at my side I don't have to worry about you."

"Don't worry, Reverend," Jack said over a mouthful of stew. "I'll be right beside you regardless of what happens."

Satisfied, the reverend smiled and asked Jack, "How is the stew?"

"It's great," Jack said, still wolfing it down.

The reverend got a bowl of stew from the steaming pot and sat down on a stump next to Jack. "Did you notice those rocky peaks high up on the mountain when we rode up this evening?"

"Yeah, I saw them," Jack replied. "What about them?"

"Look at them now in the evening sunlight," Reverend Gipson said, pointing to the tall peaks at the top of the mountains. Jack looked at the peaks and shrugged his shoulders.

"I don't see anything," he told the reverend.

"Just stare at the rocky cliffs, not looking at anything in particular," the reverend told him. Jack put down his bowl and stared at the mountaintop.

"I still don't see anything!" he said in a frustrated voice.

"You're trying too hard," the reverend told him, "relax and let the picture unfold." Jack looked at the evening shadows falling across the rocks and the glowing sky above them. He could see dark timber on one side and along the bottom of the peak. Just when he thought the reverend must be crazy, he saw a wolf's head appear seemingly out of nowhere. It was there all along—he just never allowed himself to see it. A combination of rocks, shadows, and trees made up the wolf's head, sitting like a crown on the tall peaks. Startled, he turned and looked at the reverend.

"You saw it, didn't you?" the reverend said in a quiet voice.

"What does it mean?" Jack asked, unable to take his eyes off it now that he had finally seen it.

"It can't mean anything to speak of," the reverend replied. "It was there before the wolf tribe even existed, I would imagine. You can't see

9

it during the day. I only noticed it this evening when the shadows were just right."

"Didn't Running Bear say the wolf people turned into demons at night?" Jack asked, fear in voice. "It sure seems funny the wolf's head can only be seen just before sundown."

"It does seem strange, I guess," the reverend told Jack as he ate his stew. "I wouldn't worry about it much, it's probably just something to keep the legend alive."

"Probably so," Jack replied. "Well, I better get on guard duty before Aaron comes looking for me." Grabbing his rifle, he strode away from the fire towards a group of trappers standing next to the grazing horses. As Reverend Gibson watched Jack walk away, he ate the last of his stew, reached into his possibles bag, and removed a silver musket ball. Slowly he turned the ball in his fingers as he studied the wolf's head on the mountaintop, now disappearing in the dim light. As darkness fell, he put the musket ball back in his bag and checked to make sure the other ball was there also. Relieved to know he still had them both, he looked down at his loaded rifle. He had loaded the third silver ball in his rifle before they left the river camp. He still felt foolish about the silver musket balls, but he remembered the seriousness in Running Bear's face when he told them the shiny rock would kill the wolf people forever. He wanted to give Jack one of the musket balls but was worried it would scare Jack unnecessarily. Picking up his bowl he went back to the simmering pot and filled it with more stew.

As darkness blanketed the mountainside, Jack helped bring in the horses and then went back out to where Aaron had shown him to stand guard. There was a full moon creeping up over the horizon. *They were approaching the wolf people's land during the full moon*, Jack thought, realizing their bad luck as he watched the moon rise. He sure hoped the reverend and the others knew what they were doing. Seeing the wolf's head high up on the peaks tonight was weird and seemed almost like an omen. A light breeze was blowing down off the mountain and Jack pulled the collar up on his jacket to keep out the cold. As the moon grew higher and higher in the sky, Jack could see his shadow falling across the ground. The mountain was lit up by the moon's light and Jack could see the black forest covering the mountainside. As the moon got higher the breeze went away and everything became very quiet. Jack could see the picketed horses and several campfires down below him surrounded by trappers. He watched as the trappers left the fires one by one to turn in for the night.

The quiet of the night was broken when a huge grizzly bear ran out of the timber several hundred yards below Jack. At first as he brought up his rifle, he thought it was a cow moose but then he heard it woof and whimper as it dived into the small creek and out the other side. It was scared and kept looking back over its shoulder as it ran. In the dim moonlight Jack had to strain his eyes to watch the bear run over the sagebrush ridge and disappear into the plains below. Then he saw them. Chasing the bear were four large wolves. They crossed the creek and raced up the ridge, starting to gain on the bear. At the top of the ridge one wolf stopped while the others continued on. It turned and looked briefly towards Jack with fiery yellow eyes. Jack felt the piercing stare of the wolf before it turned and ran over the ridge after the others. He had never seen yellow eyes like that on any animal and never heard of wolves chasing a grizzly bear many times their size. He went immediately into the camp and shook the reverend awake.

"What is it Jack?" the reverend said, rubbing sleep from his eyes.

"Reverend, I just saw four wolves chase a huge grizzly bear out of the forest and into the plains. But that's not the worst of it. One wolf stopped and looked at me with fiery yellow eyes."

"Are you sure you weren't dreaming again?" the reverend asked.

"No, I saw it just like I said," Jack answered in a frightened voice.

Reverend Gipson looked at Jack and could tell he was frightened. Suddenly, the silence of the night was broken by a bloodcurdling howl. Trappers scrambled from their blankets, rifles ready.

"What was that?" one trapper asked. They heard the howl again, this time farther away.

"All right, it's probably only a marauding wolf, but we had better get ready just in case. Everybody up and guard the stock!" the reverend yelled. He followed Jack to where Jack had seen the terrified grizzly.

"It went over that ridge, with the wolves close behind," Jack said pointing to the ridge. Standing there in the moonlight, they could hear howling high up on the mountaintop. It sounded like a large pack of wolves hunting in the darkness.

Everyone stood guard the rest of the night, listening to the spine-tingling howls high up on the mountain. Several hours before sunrise, Jack woke the reverend, who had dozed off for a minute.

"Look, look!" Jack told him in an excited voice, pointing to where the bear had crossed the creek. Reverend Gipson saw four sets of fiery yellow eyes running back towards the timber. He could barely see the outline of the animals. They were large for wolves, but he was sure that must be what they were. They ran in a loping gait that seemed more human than wolf. He could feel their piercing eyes as they entered the timber and disappeared.

"Did you see that?" Jack asked in astonishment.

"Yes, I believe I did," the reverend answered.

"Reverend, did you notice how they didn't run like wolves?" Jack asked in a frightened voice.

"It was probably the dim moonlight playing tricks on our eyes," the reverend answered, trying to calm Jack. "It will be daylight soon," the reverend told him. "Maybe after we ride up on the mountain and see the wolf people, we will laugh at the thought of people turning into wolves." Both men laughed and tried to hide their fear. "Take this," Reverend Gipson said holding out his hand,

"What is it?"

"It's a musket ball I cast from silver," the reverend replied. "Take it and make sure it's loaded in your rifle before we head up the mountain," Reverend Gipson told him in a serious tone. "Don't tell anyone about the silver musket ball, I don't want to be the laughingstock of all the men when we find out the wolf people are only men like us." Swearing secrecy, Jack made sure his rifle was loaded with the silver ball.

"By God, I'm glad morning finally got here," a trapper snarled as he saddled his horse. "I hate sitting in the dark, giving the wolf people more credit than they deserve. It's time to skin this wolf legend!" he yelled to the other trappers.

Breaking camp, they rode up the mountainside, following the timber's edge. High up on the mountain face they rode into thick timber, carefully working their way to the top. At the top of the face they left the timber and rode into a wide mountain park with a large stream flowing through it. Following the stream they rode through the middle of the park. High above them, mountain peaks seem to jut out from everywhere. The mountain country was huge and extended for miles. Following the stream they came to a place where it forked into two smaller creeks. The country looked like prime beaver country and everyone was excited. They started to forget the wolf people.

Aaron rode up next to the reverend and said, "We need to explore each of these drainages. This country is larger then we thought." Knowing he was right, the reverend divided their group. Half would follow Aaron and take the right fork while the rest would follow the reverend up the left fork. Agreeing to meet by noon the next day regardless of what happened, the two groups rode away from each other. It wasn't long before they were miles apart following the creeks into canyons and wide meadows. Before they split up Reverend Gipson made sure Jack was with him. Jack wanted to go with Aaron and take the drainage that seemed to go towards the wolf head peak, but Rev. Gipson told him he would know soon enough about the wolf people.

Aaron was a big man, wearing a leather fringe jacket with a soft hunting shirt underneath. He wore fringed buckskin pants tucked into tall boots. Riding a big bay horse, he led his party of trappers up the mountain stream. He had a wide-brimmed hat pulled down tightly over his long blond hair. His full beard hung down on his broad chest. With a wide face, his green eyes seem to hide behind his large nose. Nudging his horse with his heels, he led his party at a fast walk along the crystal blue flowing water of the stream. For the rest of the morning and the early afternoon they rode through the timber, following the stream, which seemed to be getting wider. As they came out of the timber Aaron saw stretched out before them a wide mountain valley. The stream they were following wound its way back and forth across the valley. In the middle of the valley the trappers saw what they had been looking for. Huge beaver dams and ponds were scattered along the valley floor.

"By God, thar's what we came here for!" Aaron said to a burly trapper who rode up next to him. Excited about the beaver sign, Aaron forgot about the wolf people and the danger they represented. Red bunches of tall willows covered in green leaves grew thick along the winding stream. Aaron led his trappers up the valley, stopping to water their horses at a large beaver pond. Remembering the wolf people, Aaron quickly mounted his pony and stood guard as the others quenched their thirst. Once the group had watered, he led them towards the upper end of the valley.

"We will make camp there," he said, pointing to the lush valley floor next to the timber. Crossing the creek between beaver ponds, he led the trappers to where they would have good grass and water for their horses. Hearing something rush by his head, he turned to see an arrow strike the trapper behind him in the chest.

"Ambush!" he screamed as he turned his pony away from the timber. Arrows filled the air around them, striking both horses and men. He heard several rifle shots as he galloped away. Leading the trappers charging back across the creek and out into the open valley, he saw painted warriors attacking from the timber surrounding the valley. Riding into the middle of the valley the trappers were met by warriors hiding in the willows.

"We're trapped!" Aaron yelled as he rode away from the creek and out in the open. Pulling his horse to a stop, he could see they were surrounded.

"Shoot your horses and throw up a barricade!" he screamed as he pulled his pistol and killed his horse. Other trappers led their ponies up next to his and killed them. Soon they had a nice barricade thrown up around them, made from horseflesh and dirt. Quickly Aaron aimed his rifle at a charging warrior and fired. The warrior flung his arms high in the air and pitched headfirst to the ground. Trappers all around him were firing their rifles and with each warrior they knocked down, the others seemed to slow up until the attack had stopped. Aaron quickly reloaded and killed another warrior before he could take cover. Then just as suddenly as it had started, the attack was over.

"Where are they?" a trapper asked in despair.

"They are still out there," Aaron answered. "Watch for movement in the tall grass." As he peeked over his horse, an arrow buried itself deeply into his saddle. Seeing a warrior in the grass, Aaron sat up and quickly shot him. As he dove back behind his dead horse, he heard the warrior scream, thrash in the grass, and then lay still. As Aaron reloaded again, he looked around the barricade at the trappers. Several had been hit by arrows and lay gasping in pain. He saw several others pull the arrows from their comrades trying to ease their pain. He looked over at the creek about one hundred yards away. After dark he would get water for the wounded who were already pleading for a drink.

As the trappers lay there looking down their rifle barrels over their horse's sides, one man yelled, "Well, from what I've seen so far, my rifle doesn't have any trouble killing these wolf warriors." Aaron agreed—he had killed three of the wolf tribe without any trouble.

The sun was starting to set above the mountaintop and Aaron told his men, "All we have to do is hold out until tomorrow, when the reverend and the others will arrive. We will just stay put and get even with the wolf people then." As darkness began to fall across the valley, Aaron heard a wolf howl loudly.

The reverend was leading his group of trappers from one beaver pond to another when they heard rifle shots far away on the mountainside.

"It sounds like Aaron and the others have run into trouble!" the reverend told his men as he turned his pony and listened.

"That way!" Jack told the reverend, pointing to the top of the mountain. Reverend Gipson looked at the sun just above the horizon.

"We only have about an hour of daylight left," he told the group. "We will ride to the top of that ridge and camp for the night. Hopefully Aaron and the others can hold out until we get there tomorrow. I don't want to travel in the dark on this mountain until I know more about the wolf people."

Riding hard, they got to the top of the timbered ridge just as the sun disappeared below the mountaintops.

As the moon slowly rose higher in the dark sky, Aaron could hear more wolves howling all around them. The soft glow of moonlight lit up the valley. Aaron could see shadows running back and forth next to the timber. The terrible howling was all around them now. Aaron froze in fear as he watched the shadow of a warrior he had killed rise from the ground and howl at the moon, turning into a hideous wolf creature with fiery yellow eyes. Coming to his senses, he tried to shoot the wolf demon but it turned and was gone. Desperately he searched the moonlight for the demon but couldn't find it.

"Hey, the Indian I shot is gone!" a trapper across from Aaron muttered in disbelief. A trapper screamed and fired his rifle at something in the darkness. Aaron turned to see a demon with yellow eyes and sharp teeth suddenly appear in front of the screaming trapper. The wolf demon bit the big man on his shoulder and easily dragged him over his horse and away into the darkness. Rushing to the man's horse, Aaron tried to get a shot at the wolf demon, but it was gone. The night air was filled with the hideous screams of the trapper being dragged away in the darkness. Wolves were howling all around them and Aaron could see their fiery yellow eyes circling the trappers in the dark. Aaron and the men were terrified after watching the wolf demon drag their friend away.

"What do we do?" a trapper said in a broken, frightened voice.

"Do the best you can," Aaron yelled back. "Don't give up!" A terrible growl was followed by a wolf leaping over the horse barricade. Standing on its hind legs, it growled and showed its large teeth. It was covered in fur and had the head, ears, and teeth of a wolf. Its body was more human-like but terribly misshapen. It had long terrible claws on its front paws that resembled hands. Aaron saw it look at him with its evil, yellow eyes as he shot it with his rifle, as did several other trappers at point-blank range. As the rifle balls hit its body, the wolf growled in anger. Leaping on one of the trappers, he grabbed the man by the neck with its powerful jaws, biting his head off. Blood squirted everywhere as the wolf picked the body up and leaped over the barricade, back into the darkness. One trapper became so crazy with fear he jumped up and ran into the darkness away from where the demon had fled. Almost instantly the trappers could hear him screaming as wolves tore him to pieces. The wounded trappers in the barricade pleaded with the others to shoot them before the wolves came for them. Terrible, murderous howling was all around them now. Aaron saw the wolf demons circling closer and closer. One trapper after another was dragged away screaming into the darkness.

The trapper's head was still lying next to Aaron. Looking into its blank eyes, Aaron became so frightened he started to lose his senses. Standing, he swung his rifle as a club, trying desperately to brain anything that came close. Yellow eyes and wicked teeth were everywhere now as wolves poured over the barricade. All around him he saw wolves attacking his friends. The night was filled with terrible screaming and growling. Aaron felt a wolf demon jump on his back and pull him to the ground. He felt terrible pain as teeth tore at his back and neck. Fighting for his life, he turned to see the wolf lunge for his throat. The yellow eyes were inches away from his own terrified eyes, when suddenly everything went dark.

Reverend Gipson heard a few more rifle shots after it got dark and knew that Aaron and his men were still alive. He hoped they would get to Aaron in the morning in time to save them. They heard howling everywhere on the mountain all night. As the night wore on, the howling was concentrated high up on the mountain. *Maybe Aaron and his bunch had driven the wolf people away, chasing them to the mountaintop*, he thought to himself. It took forever for the sun to lighten the early-morning sky enough for the trappers to move out. Reverend Gipson had the men saddle up and was riding down the canyon towards where he guessed the gunshots had come from as soon as it was light enough. They rode quickly but cautiously aware that whatever attacked Aaron and his men might be anywhere. By midmorning they looked down on a lush, wide-open valley with beaver ponds scattered along its bottom.

"I'm sure this is the place the rifle shots came from," Jack told the reverend. "What is that?" he exclaimed pointing to the middle of the valley.

"It looks like dead horses," the reverend replied. Quickly they rode down into the valley, rifles ready. Reverend Gipson kept his main body of trappers back and sent one of his trusted scouts in to check out the dead horses. They were still several hundred yards from the dead animals and couldn't see any signs of life. The scout approached on horseback cautiously, rifle ready across the pommel of his saddle. Stopping at the barricade his horse snorted and spooked as it caught the scent of death and wolves. The trapper looked in terror at the sight of the massacre. Controlling his fear he rode around the barricade and down to the creek. All around, he saw moccasin tracks and huge wolf tracks. Circling the site again he determined it was safe and called the reverend and the others in.

As Reverend Gipson rode up, he saw blood in the grass before he got to the horse barricade. This must be where the wolf warriors were shot and were later carried away, he told himself. Riding up to the barricade he was met by a terrible sight. Blood was everywhere, covering the dead horses and the ground inside. He saw the severed head of one of his friends, staring blankly into the sky. Dismounting, he turned to see Jack ride away several yards and vomit. Wolf tracks, large ones, were all around the barricade and on the inside. They were huge and looked more like tracks made by men standing on the balls of their feet. The grass all around the barricade was covered in dried blood. In one corner, inside the barricade, was a foot bitten off at the ankle and in another spot, a hand bitten off at the wrist.

"Where are the rest of the men Aaron had with him?" Reverend Gipson said in a broken voice. Several trappers rode away from the massacre site and returned, saying all the wolf tracks seemed to be leading back towards the mountaintop.

"Also," a trapper told the reverend, "it looks like they took the bodies of our people with them." Puzzled, Reverend Gipson remembered what Running Bear had said about the cave where the demon wolves gather to eat the dead and living.

"That must be it!" he yelled out loud, "it's time for revenge!" he told the trappers. "We will track the demons back to their cave and kill them!" Excited, he led the trappers up the mountain, following the wide blood trail. As he followed the trail, Reverend Gipson tried to think of how to kill the wolf people. Running Bear said only silver in their heart would work. He had to think of another way. Maybe if they could chase them into their cave—if there was one—they could blast the entrance shut, trapping them inside. It was a long shot but was the only thing that might work. If they didn't deal with the wolf people quickly, as soon as it got dark, they would fall prey to the wolf demons the same way Aaron's men had.

Tashina

They followed the bloody trail up and over a lightly-timbered ridge. At the top of the ridge they saw an Indian village of thirty or more tepees. Drawing their weapons, the trappers charged down off the ridge and into the village. The village appeared to be empty as the trappers rode up and dismounted, searching all the tepees. Jack followed Reverend Gipson into one large teepee and saw the reverend shoot an old warrior as he entered. Not finding anyone else in the tepee the reverend left to reload his rifle. Jack turned to follow when he saw a movement under a buffalo robe. Rifle ready, he jerked the robe away and almost shot the beautiful Indian maiden in his dreams. She was more beautiful than he remembered. She looked frightened and held her tiny hand up to protect herself from his rifle.

Lowering his rifle, Jack looked into her fawn-like black eyes. Smiling at him, she reached out to take his hand. Remembering his dreams, he pulled his hand back. Overcome by her beauty, he reached out and took her hand. Quickly he led her to the door of the teepee and checked to see if it was safe outside.

Reverend Gipson quickly reloaded his rifle. Realizing their only chance was to catch the wolf tribe in the cave, he rushed ahead, forgetting about Jack.

"Foller me!" he yelled to the trappers. Mounting their ponies they rushed up the mountain following the bloody trail. Galloping up the mountainside, they hadn't gone far when Reverend Gipson saw a large cave opening at the bottom of one of the rocky peaks. As the trappers charged the cave, Reverend Gipson saw several warriors and women run into the cave opening, warning those inside.

"Keep them in the cave!" the reverend yelled. Dismounting, the trappers fired at the cave opening, keeping everyone from escaping.

"Keep firing!" the reverend yelled. He knew the rifle balls would ricochet off the rock walls, doing terrible damage to those within. If they were lucky the shooting would drive the wolf people back farther into the cave. Running to a packhorse, the reverend removed the two kegs of gunpowder.

"Cover me!" he yelled to his men as he climbed the mountain to get to the entrance. Arrows were flying wildly from the mouth of the cave, shot by bows too far back to see what they were shooting at. Running to the cave opening, the reverend took a quick shot at a warrior fleeing deeper inside the cave. The cave entrance was huge and the reverend knew his powder kegs couldn't blow it shut. He would need to get the kegs farther down in the cave to do any good. Calling his men up, he had them concentrate their fire into the cave. All morning and into the afternoon they continued their standoff. Rev. Gipson knew the wolf people were just waiting for nightfall to turn into demon wolves and storm the cave entrance. It was a stalemate and there was only about three hours of daylight left. If he didn't do something soon, they would all die!

"If the wolf people turn into demon wolves, our rifles won't hold them in the cave and we will be destroyed!" he told the trappers. "There is only one thing to do!" Picking up a powder keg under each arm, he turned to look at the blue sky one last time, and ran headlong down into the cave. As he raced into the cave, he saw human body parts scattered on the floor. *He was right*, he thought to himself as he ran farther into the cave, *they were all gathered at the back of the cave waiting for dark and the full moon*. The wolf people were startled to see him, but then shot arrows at the madman charging towards them. The first arrow hit the reverend in the thigh as the second arrow struck him in his shoulder. Falling to the ground, he quickly broke the bottom of one keg open using the butt of his pistol. Smiling at the attacking warriors, he fired his pistol into the gunpowder. A thunderous boom that belched black smoke and dust out of the cave entrance followed the flash from the pistol. Pulling back, the trappers saw huge boulders begin to fall deep inside the cave entrance. Then the rocky mountainside covered the cave entrance completely.

"He done it!" a trapper yelled.

"Yes he did!" another replied. "He gave his life to save us and now it's up to us to leave this evil place as fast as we can. Who knows if all the wolf people were in the cave or not?" The frightened trappers had seen enough of this mountain to last a lifetime. They scampered to their horses and rode back to the village.

Jack saw the trappers following Reverend Gipson as he told the maiden to get her belongings and he would take her where she would be safe. "What is your name?" he asked her as she gathered her stuff.

"My name Tashina," she replied.

"My name is Jack," he told her.

"Jack," she said smiling at him as he helped her carry her belongings.

"We must hurry before they return," he told her. Tying her belongings to a packhorse left behind, he mounted his pony and then reaching down, took her tiny hand and pulled her up behind him. She held tightly to his waist with her head resting on his back as he turned his pony and rode towards the top of the mountain, away from the rocky peaks. Tashina glance down at the dead old warrior as they rode out of the village and her black eyes turned fiery yellow for a split-second. Jack was determined to save her as he prodded his horse up the mountain. Suddenly the ground shook and spooked his horse. He heard a muffled boom just before the ground trembled. *Reverend Gipson must have blasted the cave shut*, he thought to himself. Tashina turned her head and saw the dust from a rockslide high upon the mountain.

"Don't worry," he said in a tender voice. "Everything is going to be all right. We will hide high up on the mountain for a few days until things cool down some." Prodding his pony, he urged it up the mountain.

The trappers rode into the village and quickly ransacked all the tepees before they set them on fire. Taking what they could carry on their saddle horses and packhorses, they burned everything else.

"It will be dark in less than an hour!" a trapper yelled. "I'm leaving this wolf country and not coming back. There's not enough beaver in the world to keep me on this mountain with those demon wolves." Everyone was still frightened and mounting up, followed the trapper down the mountain. A large black column of smoke was climbing high in the sky from the burning village. They continued to ride hard down the trail, not stopping when it got dark.

"We have to make it to where we camped the first night!" one trapper told the others. In the darkness they slowed their ponies to a walk, allowing them to pick their way carefully down the mountainside. Suddenly a terrible howl broke the silence of the night.

Jack and Tashina rode hard up the side of the mountain until they reached a small open park, surrounded by thick timber. Dismounting, Jack helped Tashina down and said, "We will stay here tonight, this place looks safe and there is good grass for our horses." She stayed close to him, not wanting to leave the safety of his presence. He looked down into her frightened eyes and held her close, telling her not to worry.

"We should leave this place," she told him in a frightened voice.

"I'm not leaving you now that I have found you. You are the woman in my dreams and for some reason I feel as if we are destined to be together," he exclaimed, holding her close. Pulling back from him, she looked deep into his eyes and told him she had dreamed of him also. Reaching into his possibles bag, Jack removed the silver wolf emblem on the chain. Tashina gasped and covered her mouth with her hands, muffling her screech of surprise.

"That is the emblem I saw in my dream," she told him in disbelief.

"Are you sure?" he asked, letting it dangle from the chain.

"Yes, you wore it around your neck for protection," she told him in an excited voice.

"Protection from what?"

"From my people. It's made of the sacred stone that can destroy us. You must wear it around your neck to protect yourself at night," she said in an excited voice. Taking it from him she held it gingerly, opening the locking clasp. Standing on her tiptoes she leaned against him and fastened it around his neck. "In my dream, this emblem of the shiny metal will protect you from the terror of the wolves," she said in a calmer voice. "Don't ever take it off while you are in these mountains," she warned him reaching out and taking his hand. "Thank you for rescuing me," she said, as she reached up and kissed his cheek.

Blushing, she turned away and told him she would make a fire before darkness fell.

Jack was floating in a dream after the kiss and barely had enough sense about him to hobble the horses and turn them out to graze. He sat at the edge of the open park watching the horses graze on the green grass as darkness fell over the mountainside. He watched Tashina working around the campfire and wondered why they had both dreamed of each other. *She was so beautiful and delicate*, he thought. They would stay here until tomorrow and then sneak back to the village and see what had happened. From the columns of black smoke rising high in the sky, he knew the village was burning. Tashina had seen it also and he saw the pain in her eyes as she realized what the smoke was from. The moon was coming up over the horizon now and the sky was full of bright stars. Glancing back towards the fire he couldn't see Tashina anywhere. Maybe she had to go in the trees for a minute, he told himself under his breath. As he watched for her return he played with the wolf emblem she had fastened around his neck. Suddenly the quiet was shattered by a bloodcurdling howl very close by. Startled, Jack searched the darkness for any signs of yellow eyes or shadows. His rifle was still loaded with the silver musket ball Reverend Gipson had given him. Then he heard the howl again farther down the mountain.

"At least," he mumbled, "it is going away from us." He was shaking and his heart felt like it was going to burst from his chest, he was so scared. Turning to look for Tashina he saw she still hadn't returned to the fire. Wherever she was, he knew she was just as afraid as he was. Maybe he should go try to find her, but where would he look in the dark timber? Then the wolf howled again much farther down the mountain than before.

Stopping their horses, the trappers looked wide-eyed into the darkness when the terrible howl broke the silence again, so close it made their skin crawl. Panicking, one trapper fired his rifle into the night.

"I saw it, I saw it!" he screamed.

"Hold your fire!" a trapper named Sam exclaimed as another rifle exploded. Sam turned his pony and saw fiery yellow eyes leap out of the darkness and a wolf-like creature pull a trapper from his horse with ease, tearing out the screaming man's throat. He quickly raised his rifle and shot the beast solidly in the chest as it sprang for him. He heard the rifle ball slam into the beast but it never slowed down at all. In an instant it leaped onto the back of his frightened horse and had its terrible jaws around his neck, dragging him screaming from his pony. When he hit the ground he was gone, spilling his life's blood onto the grass. In sheer terror, frightened horses bolted down the mountain trail. One horse reared on its hind legs, striking out at the wolf demon with its front hooves before bolting off after the others. As the horse reared, its rider froze in fear tumbled off the back of the pony. Dazed, the trapper got to his hands and knees in time to see the hideous wolf monster standing over him.

Holding up his hand to shield himself he yelled, "Don't kill me, don't kill me!" in a terrified voice. Struggling to his knees he saw the terrible yellow eyes only inches from his face. Savagely, the wolf demon grabbed him by his shoulders and lifted him easily, high in the air. He could feel the terrible claws piercing his shoulders as the wolf growled deeply and tore open his chest with its teeth. Tearing out the man's heart the wolf gulped it down and savagely threw the corpse to the ground. Lifting its evil head towards the sky it let out a spine-tingling howl. Dropping to all fours, the demon raced after the fleeing trappers.

As the terrified ponies and trappers raced down off the mountain at a breakneck speed in the dark, one of the packhorses stumbled and fell. Squealing, the pony tried to get to its feet as horses crashed into it, throwing themselves and their riders to the ground. In a tangled mess, horses were screaming and men were cussing. Getting to their feet the shaken ponies raced down the mountainside, more frightened than before. The trappers tried to catch their ponies but the frightened horses bolted over the top of them to escape.

"Now what do we do?" one of the three horseless trappers exclaimed, as he tried to find his rifle in the moonlight.

"Run," another trapper yelled pointing up the trail at the yellow eyes. "Run!"

"Wait, I can't find my rifle," the trapper yelled back.

"Forget your rifle," the other two yelled in unison as they raced down the trail on foot. Searching madly on his hands and knees the trapper found his rifle. Relieved, he cocked his rifle calmly and kneeling on one knee aimed at the fiery yellow eyes almost upon him. At the sound of the rifle shot the wolf demon was upon him, easily taking his life. The demon was covered in blood as it savagely tore at the trapper's corpse. Lifting its head high in the air it howled again before loping off after the others. The two trappers on foot were running as hard as they possibly could when they heard the savage howl.

"It's close!" the trapper in the lead screamed. "Run faster!" They hadn't gone far when the trapper running behind heard the wolf. Terrified, he looked over his shoulder and saw the terrible yellow eyes.

"It's right behind me!" he screamed. The trapper in the lead ran even faster until he thought his lungs were going to explode. He knew his friend had fallen under the wolf demon right after he screamed to run faster. Unable to keep running, he fell to his hands and knees and gasped for breath. He was beyond fear now and the world seemed to spin in front of him. Feeling a terrible pain in his chest he fell on his back. Staring at the moon, he felt the wolf demon tearing at his body before he died.

Jack spent the night huddled under a blanket away from the fire Tashina had started. Tashina never returned and he feared for her life. As soon as it got light enough to follow her tracks he would search for her. He thought he heard several rifle shots far down the mountainside where the howling was coming from. When the sun started to creep over the horizon and cast in its light over the mountain, he was relieved. Once it was light enough, he went to the cold fire pit and searched for Tashina's tracks. He saw where she had busied herself around the campfire and that was it. Jack thought he found where she walked into the timber but he wasn't sure. The forest floor was covered with pine needles, making it hard to find any tracks. Saddling his horses, he packed up everything and decided to ride back to the wolf tribe's village. He thought if Tashina got confused or frightened she would return there.

Jack kept careful watch as he rode back towards the village for any signs of Tashina. The sun had been up for over one hour when he dismounted and tied his horses in the timber. He knew the village was just ahead and thought it would be better if he went the rest of the way on foot. Cautiously, he crept through the timber, watching closely for any signs of danger. The village wasn't burning anymore, because there was no smoke curling into the sky. At the timber's edge, he stood very still and surveyed the scene before him. All the lodges had been burnt to the ground and now were only piles of ashes. The ground around the lodges was littered with belongings the trappers had cast aside as they ransacked the village.

Then he saw Tashina on her knees next to the old warrior he had seen Reverend Gipson shoot the day before. She looked as if she was crying as he walked quietly out of the timber towards her. As he got closer he could hear her sobbing and chanting in a sad voice. She never heard him walk up to her, and when he said, "Tashina you all right?" in a gentle voice, it startled her. Instantly she turned and glared at Jack. For a second as she turned, he saw her eyes turn a fiery yellow.

"Jack," she said in a broken voice, "you startled me." Standing in front of her now, Jack noticed she was dirty and her arms and legs were bloody.

"Where did you go last night?" he asked her in a suspicious voice.

"I couldn't stand the grief of losing my father and returned to him," she said pointing to the dead warrior on the ground. She looked beautiful as she smiled at him and held her tiny hand out. "Help me up, would you Jack?" she said with a little pain in her voice. Jack looked deep into her beautiful fawn eyes and then saw what looked like a gunshot wound at the top of her shoulder next to her dainty neck.

"What's that?" he exclaimed pointing his rifle barrel at her shoulder.

"Oh, it's nothing," she told him in a seductive voice.

Quickly Jack aimed his rifle at her chest and said, "This rifle is loaded with a silver ball and if you don't want it in your heart, you had better show me that wound."

"So, that is why my father sleeps forever!" she exclaimed in anger.

"Yep, shot with a silver musket ball in the heart yesterday and today he is still dead," he told her in an excited voice. "Now show me your wound!" Slowly she reached up and untied her buckskin dress at the top of her shoulders, letting it drop down to her waist. Jack stared in shock at what looked to be at least three gunshot wounds in her chest that were almost completely healed.

"Kill me, Jack, like your kind did my father!" she told him pointing with her finger to her heart. Cocking his rifle he sighted along its barrel at her bare chest and tried to pull the trigger but just couldn't do it.

"Kill me Jack!" she exclaimed.

"I can't!" he replied. "I won't!" he exclaimed in agony. "You are the woman in my dreams. I have been searching for you and can't kill you now that I have found you!" Relieved, she relaxed, and told him his kind had killed all her tribe except for her.

"I can hear my people howling far back in our sacred cave, but they are trapped in the mountain forever."

"Tashina, I can't take your life so I will leave you here on your mountain and go far away never to return," he told her in a saddened voice. "I will protect you by never telling anyone what has happened here. Did any of the others escape you last night?"

As she pulled her dress up and tied it, she looked into his eyes and shook her head.

"I thought that might be the case," he said in a quiet voice. "I'll help you bury your father and then you will never see me again."

"I am alone now Jack," she told him in a tender voice. "You have been in my dreams for several moons. I sense there is something special between us and wish that you would stay with me in what will be our country." Then she held her small hand out to him again. They smiled at each other and Jack reached out. Taking her dainty hand, helped her to her feet.

"Go get cleaned up," he told her, kissing her cheek. "I will start to prepare your father for burial." He watched her as she walked to the stream below the village. Removing her dress, she washed the dirt and blood from the night's work off her body.

Jack wrapped the warrior in a buffalo robe he found, and when Tashina was done washing, she showed him where to build the burial scaffold. Tashina found some of her father's belongings scattered around in the village and placed them next to his side on the scaffold. Returning to the village they gathered everything worth keeping.

"With what we have been able to find we should have enough warm clothes to get us through the freezing winter," Tashina told him, smiling. "This is where I want our lodge to be," she told Jack pointing to the center of the village. "My people have stayed in this spot since the beginning of time. Our children will grow strong in the land of their people," she told Jack, pointing at the surrounding mountains.

"Tashina, how will you and I live together when you turn into a wolf during the full moon?"

Tashina thought for a moment and then said, "Your wolf emblem will protect you from me at first. As our love for each other grows I hope to be able to overcome my wild instincts and hunt my prey on the mountain's far side when the moon is full." Wrapping her arms around him, she held him tightly and whispered in his ear she could never hurt the man in her dreams. Satisfied, Jack told her he would build a warm cabin for them to live in where she wanted it, in the middle of the village. Returning to his horses, Jack brought them back to the village and left the packhorse with Tashina.

"I'm going to ride down the mountain and see if I can find any supplies or anything else we can use."

"Jack," Tashina said as he started to ride away, "what you see as you ride down the mountain, the wolf inside me did. I am both evil and good," she told him, placing her hand on his knee as she stood next to his horse. "Terrible things happened where you are going but remember wonderful things can happen also if you stay as my husband," she told him in a gentle voice. "I am the last of the wolf people," she said in a sad voice, "our children will keep my people alive. If you choose not to return I will understand," she told him, stepping away from the side of his horse.

Smiling, Jack said, "I'll be back before dark," and rode away. Tashina watched him go and felt a pang of fear in her heart that he might not return. In her dreams he saved her people from vanishing forever. *She must build a cooking fire and prepare some food*, she thought to herself. She was not hungry after feeding the last several nights but she knew that Jack would be if he returned.

Jack followed the trail down the mountainside for almost an hour before he came upon the first gruesome scene. Blood and body parts were everywhere as he dismounted and searched the clothing for anything he might be able to use. Feeling sick, he collected the rifles and all the shot and powder he could find. Placing them where he could pick them up later, he tried to vomit but couldn't. His horse was wide-eyed and spooky from the blood and wolf smell as he quickly mounted and continued down the trail. His stomach still felt sick and he felt clammy and weak. He couldn't believe someone as dainty and small as Tashina could tear grown men apart like he had just seen. Suddenly, his horse jerked its head up and whinnied at something down the trail. It was a packhorse, busily munching the green grass without a care in the world. As Jack slowly approached the horse to catch it, he was relieved to see it had the dried meat packed in its panniers. Talking gently to the pony, he reached out and grabbed the lead rope. Tying the pony to a stout tree he continued down the mountain.

As he found more gruesome corpses and body parts scattered along the trail, his body screamed to ride far away from this mountain as fast as he could. He knew Tashina would not follow him, he could tell by the way she spoke to him when he left. How could he ever love an animal that could do the terrible things he had seen? He found one more packhorse and two saddle horses at the foot of the mountain. One saddle horse was crippled, holding one foot in the air. He unsaddled it and turned it loose. *The rest of the ponies must have run off into the plains*, he thought to himself as he started back up the mountain, leading the reluctant horses.

At one point he had to stop and tail the horses together, tying them one behind the other. Picking up the lone packhorse he continued up the mountain, lashing all the stuff he had found to the ponies.

"Why am I going back?" he asked himself in a muffled voice. "I can't leave her alone," he told himself. "Regardless of what kind of hideous demon she turns into." It was almost as if she had a power over him, pulling him back to her. He was frightened of her and attracted to her at the same time, and it was driving him crazy.

Tashina could smell Jack and the horses long before she saw them. She was excited he had returned and hoped what he saw wouldn't make him hate her. She helped him tend the horses after he rode up and put them out to pasture.

"Something smells good," he said as he walked to the cooking fire. On the hot coals was a simmering pot. Tashina used a horn spoon to fill a wooden bowl with the stew she had made.

"Sit down, Jack," she told him, tenderly pointing at a buffalo robe spread out next to the fire. Jack sat cross-legged on the robe as she handed him the bowl of stew and the spoon.

"This smells delicious," he told her, hearing his hungry stomach rumble.

"I made it for you."

"Aren't you going to eat any?"

"I got hungry and ate before you got back," she said, lying to him. Tasting the hot stew and liking it, Jack quickly wolfed three bowls down while Tashina watched him quietly.

"You must stay at this fire tonight," she told him in a concerned voice. "In several days the moon will be gone and I won't be bothered with the wolf. Then I will be able to spend the evening with my new husband. For now, always wear your wolf necklace and stay close to this fire." Jack could see the seriousness in her eyes as she spoke.

That night he sat next to the fire with his rifle. He had a blanket pulled over his shoulders to keep out the cold. At dusk, Tashina made sure he still wore the necklace and then ran quickly away from the village. Moments later Jack heard a loud mournful howl and knew Tashina had changed into the demon. Rifle ready just in case, he saw yellow eyes briefly at the forest edge and then they were gone. He could hear her howling down the mountainside and knew she went to eat what was left of his friends. Feeling his skin crawl, he pulled the blanket around his shoulders. One thing had been puzzling him all day. He never found Reverend Gipson's body down the mountainside and yet Tashina had told him all the trappers had died. It must mean that the reverend died at the cave when they blasted it shut. *He would miss the reverend,* he thought to himself as he closed his eyes and tried to sleep.

In the days that followed Jack and Tashina built a fine cabin and enjoyed being with each other. When the moon wasn't full in the evening sky Jack couldn't believe Tashina was part wolf. She was so kind and gentle, and he found himself thinking he must be crazy to think she could turn into something evil. Several times he had wanted to take the wolf necklace off while they were laboring on the cabin but she insisted he leave it on.

"Why?" he asked her. "There is no moon tonight."

"I know," she replied in a gentle voice. "But I still feel better knowing you have it on."

When winter came, storms and blizzards pelted their cabin but they stayed safe and warm inside. During the freezing winter nights of the full moon, Tashina would leave at dusk, telling Jack to lock the door. Jack always feared she would freeze to death, but when morning arrived he would hear her tap on the door and her tiny voice would ask to be let in. He never asked her what she did or where she went on those nights and she was always thankful for that.

As spring started to arrive, Tashina told Jack they were going to be parents. Jack was elated and then suddenly looked sober.

"Will our child be like you?" he asked her. "Or like me?"

"I'm not sure Jack," she said tenderly. "This has never happened before. If you were of my people our child would be wolf. You are not of my people, so I'm not sure what to expect."

"When you turn wolf will you hurt our child?"

"Not if the child is wolf. If it is not, I'm not sure what the demon in me will do. It would destroy me if I were to kill our child," she told him with tears in her eyes. Jack never knew what to hope for; he just hoped the mother and child would be healthy and fine after the delivery.

When the day came for Tashina to have their child, Jack was relieved. The phases of the moon had just passed and Tashina was free to concentrate on having her baby. She labored almost a full day before the baby arrived. It was a son and both parents were ecstatic. The baby was healthy and so was Tashina. They named their new son Chato after Tashina's father. That night while Tashina was nursing her son, Jack brought her a bowl of stew he had made.

"Sit it there and I'll eat it once it cools," she told him, smiling, as she cradled her son. "What's wrong?" she asked, seeing worry on her husband's face.

"Is our son like you or like me?" he asked her in a shaky voice.

"I can't tell yet." She saw how worried he looked. "Maybe as he gets older I can tell," she said kissing Chato on his forehead. "Don't worry, as long as you wear the wolf emblem and stay in the cabin with our son, the wolf in me will stay away." As the weeks passed, Tashina told her husband her son was both like her people and like his father.

"What do you mean?" Jack asked her.

"He is wolf as well as like you."

"Is he safe to be around you when you are wolf?"

"I'm not sure," she replied, "I've never been around anyone like him before."

They worked hard that spring and summer preparing for the coming winter. Chato was growing fast but Tashina could still not tell if he would be safe with her or not. Her mother's instinct said yes, but she would not risk her son's life to find out.

One night when the moon was full, Jack sat safely in the cabin playing with Chato. He had heard Tashina howl several times close to the cabin. Usually she went as far as possible right away, but he noticed since Chato had been born the wolf in her stayed close by. Fall was in the air and there was a chilly breeze blowing.

As the fire in the cabin started to die down, Jack remembered he had forgotten to bring firewood in before dark. The cabin was already starting to get cold and he knew it would get much colder by morning without a fire. The last time he heard Tashina howl she was farther away from the cabin so he thought it would be safe for him to quickly run to the woodpile and back. Putting on his coat, he grabbed his rifle and started to unlock the door. He wouldn't be able to lock the door when he left and that would leave Chato unprotected. Seeing his son playing on the robe spread out on the floor in the dying firelight, he removed his wolf necklace. Going to Chato, he tied the necklace around his tiny waist. It would just be for a few seconds, he told himself, and then he would be back inside with an armload of firewood. Pulling his collar up, he unlocked the door and quickly stepped outside, shutting the door behind him.

The breeze was cold as he walked quickly to the woodpile. Leaning his rifle on the woodpile, he quickly loaded his arms full of wood. Turning to reach for his rifle and go in, he dropped the wood in shock of what he saw standing before him. Tashina stood before him in all her demon glory. Her terrible yellow eyes looked deep into his eyes. She was huge, standing there on her hind legs, growling, as saliva dripped from her white fangs. Jack slowly reached for his rifle and brought it up to his shoulder. The wolf demon acted hesitant, not knowing what to do. Cocking his rifle he aimed at the demon's heart and then remembered his small son in the cabin. Unable to shoot, he lowered the rifle and leaned it against the woodpile.

"Tashina," he said softly. "It's me Jack." The demon's ears pointed forward listening to his voice when the cocked rifle slid down off the woodpile and went off. In an instant the wolf was on him ...

Silver

A young man walked up the steps and into the general store.

"Excuse me," he said to the store clerk busy putting groceries on a shelf. "Can you tell me where I can get this weighed and valued?"

"Let me see that, young man," the clerk said, taking the rock of ore from his hand. Adjusting his spectacles to see better, he whistled quietly. "This is silver!" he exclaimed. "One of the purest veins I have ever seen." Looking over the top of his wire-rimmed glasses he asked, "Where did you find this?" in an excited voice.

"Up on the mountain," the young man replied. "Now can you tell me where to get this valued?"

"Sure, sure," the clerk replied, handing the chunk of ore back. "Across the street and four doors down is the assay office." Nodding his head in thanks, the young man went out the door and across the street. Placing his hands on his hips the store clerk watched him enter the assay office. "There goes a rich young man," he mumbled to himself, still thinking about the pure vein of silver in the chunk of ore.

As the door to the assay office opened a bell hanging above the door jingled. Shutting the door the young man walked over to the counter and placed the chunk of ore on the countertop. An old man wearing an apron with his shirtsleeves rolled up looked up from tending a cabinet full of files.

"I'll be right there," he said, closing the file drawer and wiping his hands on his apron as he walked over to the counter. "Well, what have we got here?" he asked, reaching out and picking up the chunk of ore. Studying the silver vein the man searched the counter for a loupe and then finding it, looked at the vein again. "Uh huh, uh huh," the man muttered as he studied the vein. "Where did you find this?" he asked.

"On the mountain," the young man replied.

"Which mountain?"

"I was told you could place a value on the silver in the rock," the young man stated.

"I can do better than that. I will give you cash for this chunk of ore."

"Good," the young man replied. "I've got several more chunks in my sack here better than that one." Lifting the heavy leather sack hanging from a strap over his shoulder, he put the sack up on the counter.

"Oh my goodness," the man said in awe as he removed the chunks of ore from the sack. "Just a minute young man," he said. "I will be right back."

Running out the door the little man ran down the boardwalk to the bank. Inside the bank for only a few minutes, the man in the apron returned with a finely-dressed man in a suit. The bell jingled as the door opened to the assay office and both men entered. Returning to his side of the counter, the assay clerk introduced the man in the suit to the young man.

"I asked Sam Jenkins from the bank to help me value the silver you have brought in."

"Mr. Jenkins, I'm pleased to meet you," the young man said reaching out and shaking his hand. "My name is Chato."

"The pleasure is all mine," Mr. Jenkins replied. "Now let's look at what has got Ben here so excited." Picking up a chunk of ore he examined it. "This is certainly all that Ben told me it was," he said squinting through the loupe at the vein of silver. "I'm not going to bother asking you where you found this silver," he said setting the ore back on the table. "But I will tell you if the vein of silver you busted these chunks from runs very far at all, I can make you a very rich man!"

Chato looked deep into the man's eyes and then replied, "All I want is a fair price for the silver. To answer your question, the vein of silver is over a foot wide in spots near the surface."

"My God!" Ben exclaimed in disbelief. "As soon as word gets out about this silver you brought in today people are going to go crazy looking for where you found it."

"Mining silver can be expensive, sinking a shaft and such. Sure, you can bring a few chunks of ore to town now and then, but you risk losing it all if someone discovers where you found it. What you need is a business partner with the financial backing to invest the kind of money into the mine to make it pay big time." Wiping the sweat from his brow, the man in the suit continued. "If you take me as your partner, I will handle everything, and all you will have to do is count your money. If the silver is as wide as you say, I will split the profits with you once I have been paid for my initial investments."

Chato listened to the man in the suit talk. He could smell the cheap cologne on the man and wondered how he could stand it. Chato was a tall man with wide shoulders and narrow hips. He was dressed in buckskin pants tucked into tall moccasins. He wore a fringed hunting jacket over a homespun shirt with ties down the front. A wide leather belt was wrapped around his waist with a large knife and scabbard hanging from it. On his head was a wide-brimmed hat pulled down tightly on his raven black hair that hung down to his shoulders. His eyes were green and seemed to watch everything from behind his high cheekbones and square chin. As he listened to the banker, he toyed with a silver wolf emblem hanging around his neck on a silver chain. The banker was tall and heavyset, on the verge of overweight. Chato could tell he hadn't done much physical labor in his life. Beads of sweat were across the banker's forehead, making him look fatigued from giving Chato his speech.

"Well, what do you think Chato? You want to take me in as your partner or risk losing it all if your mine is discovered?"

"Pay me for what this silver is worth and I will take you to the spot on the mountain where I found it. If you are still interested, I will take you as my partner if my mother agrees."

"Your mother, where she now?" the banker asked.

"She is guarding the silver," Chato answered.

"I hope she will be safe until we can get there," Sam replied in a worried voice.

"She will be fine," Chato stated matter-of-factly. "You don't know my mother!" Smiling, he agreed to take Sam Jenkins with him the next morning when he returned to the mountain. Ben quickly paid him in gold coins for the silver ore on the counter and Chato told Sam he would meet him there at daylight.

Leaving the assay office, Chato crossed the street and walked back into the general store. As he walked around the store picking up supplies, the store clerk asked him how it went in the assay office.

"I already got a volunteer to be my partner if I want," Chato said in a sarcastic voice.

"Let me guess, Sam Jenkins," the clerk said as Chato put the supplies on the store counter.

"I reckon so," Chato said, laying several coins on the counter.

"Let me give you a word of advice if I may," the store clerk offered. "Be careful Sam Jenkins doesn't take it all away from you like he has with others in this town."

"Thanks for the advice," Chato told the man as he put what supplies he could into his leather sack and carried the rest in his arms, leaving the store. Walking down the street he could feel eyes watching him from store windows. He guessed the word of his discovery was already out. Going to his horses, he loaded all the supplies in the panniers. Mounting his saddle horse, Chato rode out of town leading the packhorse. *Things were going just as he and his mother had planned*, he thought to himself with a big smile. Toying with the silver wolf emblem hanging around his neck, he thought of his father. His mother often told him stories of what a fine man his father was. It had only been a couple of years now since she told him how his father had really died. She had always said before a bear had killed him.

"The night your father died," she told him, "a large piece of me died with him. Your father left the cabin to get wood and wrapped his protective charm around your waist to protect you." Tears streamed down her cheeks and she started to sob. "The demon inside me met your father before he could get back inside the cabin." Sobbing harder now, she told him, "He could have killed the wolf in me but he didn't. I tried to fight the demon inside but when his rifle slid off the woodpile and exploded I lost all control and your father died. I killed the only man I ever loved!" she sobbed. Chato wrapped his arms around her and comforted her. He wasn't surprised it had happened. He knew when he turned into the wolf demon it was very hard to control. However, he was different from his mother and her people. They turned into the wolf when the full moon rose but he could turn into the wolf at will. When the moon was full the wolf was upon his mother but the moon never bothered Chato. He could keep himself from turning into a wolf demon when the moon was full if he wanted. He could also change into the wolf when there was no moon at all.

His power was stronger than any of her people and his mother always told him he must use his power to help bring their people back. As a boy, Chato could hear the wolf people howl inside the mountain and dig with their claws at the rock walls. He tried to dig into the cave entrance but couldn't get through the huge boulders. His mother told him that a silver bullet in their hearts would destroy them forever, like it had her father. She also showed him the wolf tribe's greatest secret. A huge vein of silver could be found on the surface of the ground near the top of the mountain, and the vein continued into the mountainside. The wolf people guarded the silver, knowing it could destroy them. When Tashina showed him the silver he began to develop a plan. With her help, they decided to let the world know about this silver and sink a mineshaft into the side of the mountain. Following the silver vein the miners would unknowingly release the wolf people from their tomb. Then they would destroy the mine and everyone in it, making the mountain once again a place filled with demons.

Chato laughed to himself when he thought of how easily the banker took the bait. Finding a nice grove of trees not too far from town, Chato decided to camp for the night. He would ride in early the next morning and get the banker before riding to the mountain. As he tended his ponies, his stomach growled with hunger. Taking a piece of jerky from his pack, he chewed on it briefly before throwing it away. What he was hungry for was raw meat, he told himself as his eyes began to turn yellow.

Jacob Morris was just pulling the harness from his team of horses when his son, a boy tall for his age, yelled into the open doors of the barn.

"Pa, Ma says it's time to eat."

"Okay, tell her I'm almost done and will be in soon."

"Don't take too long. I'm starved," the boy said as he ran for the house.

"Give me a hand then," Jacob replied before he realized his son had already left. Using a lamp for light, he hung the heavy harness on the barn wall and leading the draft horses into their stalls, turned them loose. They both nickered at him as he grabbed a pitchfork and pitched loose hay into their stalls.

"Yeah, I know," he told them, "you're hungry too." Looking out the barn door he saw it was pitch black outside. He could see light shining out from the windows of the house. Smelling his wife's supper made his stomach growl with hunger pains. As he pitched the last forkful of hay to the horses, he saw something run by the open doors of the barn. Turning to see if his son had returned, a loud piercing wolf howl startled him. He almost dropped the pitchfork. The horses snorted and stared wide-eyed at the barn door. They ran to the back of their stalls and stood trembling. Jacob knew the wolf was close from the way the horses were acting. *Well, if it wanted to take him on with his pitchfork, so be it,* he thought as he walked carefully to the door. He hadn't seen a wolf around these parts for over twenty years. As he stepped toward the barn entrance he heard a deep growl just behind the barn doors.

"Get out of here!" he yelled, slamming the pitchfork on the ground ahead of him. As the growling intensified he saw a tall shadow slowly come around the side of the door. As it stepped into the lamplight, he gasped in fear. It was a wolf, standing upright, with terrible claws and teeth. The wolf's eyes were a fiery yellow and seemed to look right through him. The horses, mad with fear, bolted out the side of the barn, tearing the wall into kindling. "My God what are you?" Jacob gasped as he raised the pitchfork. Slowly the demon crept toward him. Its ears lay back on its evil head, ready to pounce. Frozen in fear, Jacob couldn't believe what was happening as the wolf suddenly charged.

Running into the pitchfork's tines, the wolf growled in anger. It pulled the fork from its chest and threw it away. Jacob wanted to run but couldn't move as the wolf demon grabbed him and began eating. He managed a loud scream and then was gone. Blood was flung everywhere as the wolf feasted on Jacob's body. As the wolf gulped down big chunks of meat, it saw the door to the house open and a boy with a rifle peek out. Grabbing the mangled corpse, the wolf vaulted the stable fence and ran out into the darkness through the hole in the side of the barn.

The next morning at daybreak, when Chato rode up to the assay office, he saw Sam Jenkins waiting. He was dressed in boots and homespun clothes and wearing a wide-brim hat. The town was busy for that early in the morning. Riders were starting to gather just down the street.

"Morning Sam," Chato said. "What's all the commotion about?"

"Oh, a farmer was killed last night by a bear. They are forming a hunting party to find the bear and kill it before anyone else gets hurt."

"Well, if we see it on the way to the mountain we will kill it for them," Chato replied with a smirk. As Chato watched Sam mount up he saw the boy he had seen last night at the house, consoling what must be his mother.

"You both were very lucky last night," he said under his breath, "that my hunger was satisfied with the man in the barn." Smacking his lips he remembered how good the raw meat tasted and his eyes turned yellow for a split-second. Turning back to Sam he smiled and said, "I hope they get the bear quickly, we sure don't want to have a killer bear following us where we are going." Laughing, he turned his horse and rode out of town with Sam Jenkins close behind. Sam trotted his pony to keep up with Chato's fast-walking horses and thought to himself how easy this was going to be. Taking the silver away from this young man and his mother would be a cinch. He almost laughed out loud when he remembered the relief on Chato's face when he mentioned being a partner and running the operation. *He would run the operation all right*, he thought smiling, *and would take every bit of the profit, too.* Chato rode hard that day and saw it had taken its toll on Sam. For supper that night Sam ate several sticks of jerky, went to his blankets, and fell asleep. Chato chewed on the jerky and watched Sam snoring in his blanket.

"It's too bad I need you," he muttered in an evil voice, "or I would feast on your fat body." Licking his lips, he imagined how tender Sam would be. Catching himself starting to turn into a wolf, he snapped himself out of it and tried to get some sleep.

Chato and Sam rode for three days along the foothills of the mountains.

"I'm starting to think we are never going to get there," Sam said, removing his hat and wiping the sweat from his forehead with a neckerchief. "How much longer until we get there?" he asked Chato in despair.

"We should be there by tomorrow night," Chato replied

"Good," Sam said. "I was going to go back if you said it would be very much longer."

"Now Sam," Chato said in a cocky voice, "you wouldn't want to do that because the bear might get you." Smiling, he turned his horse and led them up the steep mountainside. That night they camped on the side of the mountain with tall pines all around them. Sam breathed in the cool mountain air and could smell the pines in the breeze.

The next morning, Chato led them steadily up the mountainside. By early afternoon they rode into a wide valley with tall willows almost hiding the blue mountain stream winding its way down the valley. Taken by the valley's beauty, Sam asked, "How much farther?"

"Just over the ridge at the head of the valley," Chato replied

"This country is almost too beautiful to mine!" Sam exclaimed as he stood in his stirrups. Chato led the way up the valley and over the ridge, continuing to follow the stream. Once at the top of the timber ridge they saw the cabin below them on the hillside. Chato knew his mother already knew they were there. She probably smelled them several miles back. Riding down off the ridge, Chato led Sam to the cabin corrals at the edge of the timber.

"This is it," he said, jumping down from his horse and unsaddling it. Sam did the same and soon the horses were turned loose in the corral to graze on whatever grass they could find. Taking the panniers of supplies, Chato went to the house with Sam close behind and opened the door. Entering the cabin he put the supplies next to the wall and turned to Sam.

"Sit down," he said, "and I will see what I can round up for supper."

"Where is your mother?" Sam asked in a concerned voice.

"Oh, I'm sure she is around," Chato replied as he started to build a fire in the fireplace. "Here," Chato said to Sam, "take this pot and go get fresh water from the creek and we will make some coffee." Eager to help, Sam grabbed the pot and went to the creek.

The sun, just starting to set, was cradled gently by the mountaintops. Sam filled the pot and stood up.

"How are you?" a voice said. Sam was startled and almost dropped the pot. Turning, he saw a small woman smiling at him from the other side of the stream. She wore a buckskin jacket over a well-worn cloth dress that hung down to the tops of her moccasin-clad feet. Her hair was long and black with a hint of gray strands starting to show in places. Her face was beautiful as she smiled and apologized for startling him.

"You must be Chato's mother!" Sam exclaimed. "He never told me his mother was so beautiful." Blushing, she picked her way across the stream.

"My name is Tashina," she said politely.

"How do you do ma'am," Sam exclaimed. "My name is Sam Jenkins and I hope to be your new mining partner."

"Good," she told him. "The sooner we can sink a shaft and follow the silver back into the mountain the happier I will be." She laughed as she walked towards the house.

Following her, Sam admired her beauty. "This is going to be a partnership I'm going to enjoy," he muttered under his breath. He waited as Tashina went back behind the cabin and returned with several large deer steaks. Sam opened the cabin door for her and followed her inside. Chato greeted his mother and then turned the cooking chore over to her. As she laid the steaks next to the fire, Chato smiled. He could see his mother's lips were still bloody from eating a steak raw before she got back to the cabin with the others.

"How would you like your steak?" Tashina asked Sam.

"Rare," Sam replied. Tashina looked quickly at Chato and smiled as she placed the steaks over the fire.

The next morning Chato let Sam sleep in, while he and his mother went outside. "He is eager to start the mining," Chato told her.

"I'm sure he expects to get it all before he is through," Tashina replied in a wicked voice.

"Who cares what he thinks as long as he has the money to drive a shaft into the mountain and release our people?" Chato asked.

"When our people are free we will drive off everyone we don't kill," Tashina said in an angry voice. "Then once again we will be a powerful people, spreading terror in the hearts of all who live around us." Going back into the cabin, Chato woke up Sam.

"Get up, Sam, it's time to go to the silver vein." Sitting up, Sam rubbed the sleep from his eyes and got dressed. Following Chato outside, he shielded his eyes from the bright sun, pulling the brim of his hat down farther on his forehead.

"Good morning ma'am," Sam said to Tashina when he saw her standing in the sunlight. Tashina greeted him with a smile and told Chato to get a shovel. Chato got a shovel from the side of the cabin and took Sam on foot to the high plateau where the silver vein was. Sam was winded by the time they got there. Sitting on a large rock, he said he needed to rest for a while. Gasping for breath, he glanced down at the ground all around him and saw it was covered with the dark ore Chato had brought to town.

"This is the place," he said in a loud voice. "This is the place, isn't it?" Chato and Tashina both smiled and walked behind the boulder Sam was resting on.

"The vein starts here," Chato told him scraping the ground with his shovel. "It runs towards the rockslide on the side of the mountain." Excited now, Sam took the shovel and dug the dirt away from the silver vein. He could see where Chato had taken the chunks of ore that he had sold in town.

"My God, look at this!" he exclaimed, getting to his hands and knees to brush the dirt and dust off the shiny silver gleaming in the sun. "The vein is huge and appears to get wider as it goes back into the mountainside." Standing up, he dropped the shovel. Looking at Chato and Tashina, he stuck out his hand. "You have got a partner if you want one," he told them, smiling. Chato smiled at his mother and then shook Sam's hand warmly. Sam extended his hand towards Tashina and she placed her small hand in his and shook it.

"Welcome to our mine, partner," she said in a teasing voice. Sam was delighted, this was turning out much better than he had planned.

"Have you filed a silver claim on this land?" he asked both of them. To his dismay, Sam saw Chato smile and nod his head.

"We filed on this land years ago and I refilled the claim three weeks ago."

"Great," Sam yelled, thinking to himself in disgust that now he would have to be partners with them if they had already filed a claim on the land. Turning, he looked at the rockslide and saw a tunnel had been started into the huge boulders. "It looks like someone has been doing a little mining here already," he said.

"Yes, I have been working on that for years, but have only gotten that far," Chato replied.

"Well, don't worry," Sam said, rubbing his hands together. "Before you know it we will have a shaft blasted back into the mountain and a town full of miners just below your cabin. We're all going to be rich!" he told them, shaking their hands. Once back at the cabin, Sam told them he would ride back to town immediately to start getting things moving. It would take some time to move all the equipment and tools they would need to operate the mine to the mountain. They were going to need to harvest many of the tall pine trees on the surrounding hillsides in order to have enough lumber to build the mineshaft and the miner's houses. "Most of the miners would sleep in tent houses," Sam said, "which will help save some lumber. I estimate it will be mid next month before we can get everything on this mountain and start mining. In the meantime," Sam told them, "we need to load a packhorse with all the silver ore it can carry. I will take it to town and sell it, using the money to start our mining expedition." Chato led a packhorse back up to the silver vein and Sam dug out enough ore with silver in it to load the horse. Satisfied, they returned to the cabin and Sam got ready to leave.

"Well, partners," he told them as he saddled his horse and prepared to ride out, "the quicker I get to town and get the wheels in motion, the quicker we will all become rich."

"Sam," Chato said with a serious look on his face. "Watch out for that killer bear on your ride back to town. Are you sure you don't want me to go back to town with you?"

"I'll be fine," Sam said. Mounting his horse, he turned and waved at them before riding down the mountain and disappearing out of sight.

"It's a good thing he left today," Tashina told Chato. "The moon will be full again in two days and I can't control the wolf in me the way you can."

Chato smiled at her and said, "It's just as well, he is probably nothing but gristle and fat." Tashina laughed and licked her lips, wondering how good he would taste.

Mining Begins

True to his word, Sam sent a mine foreman and over a dozen miners to the mine as soon as he got back to town. Loaded down with supplies, they arrived in a long pack train two weeks after Sam left the mountain. Tashina watched them ride across the lower valley. They were bringing a pack train up the mountain with over forty mules in it. She saw Chato ride down to meet them. Sitting on the mountainside, she thought in despair how the beautiful valley would soon be filled with people of all shapes and sizes. The lush grass would soon be trampled into dust as the miner's camps covered everything. The mountain would be full of people from the town far below, eager to make money from the miners. She watched as Chato showed the miners where to start setting up their camps. She could smell the burly miners and smiled thinking of the joy the next full moon would bring.

Chato rode down off the timbered ridge and met the miners leading a long string of pack mules. The rider in the lead saw him and halted the pack train.

"You must be Chato," the rider said, extending his open hand. Chato smiled, and reaching over, saw his hand almost disappear in the huge bear-like paw of the smiling miner. "My name is Scotty," the man said in a booming voice. He was a huge man with wide, thick shoulders and thick arms and legs. He wore a heavy wool shirt with wool pants tucked into tall black leather boots. Around his waist was a wide leather belt with a large bowie knife and scabbard hanging from it. His wide face was covered with stubble, making his square chin look almost blue. His eyes were blue and practically hidden behind his thick eyebrows. His wide nose had been broken several times and seemed to almost be smashed back into his face. Chato could tell from the scars on the man's face and knuckles that he was a brawler. A well-worn derby hat made from beaver was pressed down tightly on his head, keeping his short blond hair in place. "Sam Jenkins told me to tell you he sent us as soon as he got back."

"He must have," Chato replied. "I never expected company this soon."

"Well the minute someone mentions a huge silver strike people race to find it," Scotty said, removing his hat and wiping the sweat from his brow. "I'm your new mine foreman," he said proudly. "As soon as we can get camp set up, I'm eager for you to show me where the mine will be."

"Sounds good to me," Chato said, turning his horse and pointing to the upper end of the valley. "Start setting up your camp there."

"Lead the way," Scotty said, starting the pack train moving. Chato took them to the upper end of the valley and watched them start to set up their camp. Dismounting, Scotty was stiff and smiled at Chato saying, "I'm not used to all the riding I've done the last couple days."

"When you are done setting up camp you are welcome to eat supper with us," Chato told him. "Just go to the top of that ridge and you will see the cabin. If you get there early enough, I will show you where the silver is."

"That would be great!" Scotty replied in a deep voice. "Let me get these hard-luck miners squared away and I'll be right there." Waving goodbye, Chato return to the cabin. Tashina met him at the corral when he rode up.

"It's starting," she said as he put his pony in the corral.

He saw the sad look in her eyes and knew like her that their mountain would be changed forever and asked, "Are you sure you want to go through with this?"

"Yes," she replied. "It's the only way to save our people."

"I invited the mine foreman to eat with us," he told her as they walked towards the cabin. "Oh and by the way, he is a really big man and can probably eat several big steaks."

"Good," she replied. "We need to get some prey up here with meat on their bones. I'm tired of only chasing down deer when the moon is full." Laughing, they both went inside the cabin, glad it was finally starting.

Scotty walked to the cabin after getting his men and stock taken care of. Chato and Tashina greeted him as he knocked on the cabin door.

"Scotty, this is my mother and partner in the mine, Tashina," Chato said, introducing his mother.

"How do you do, ma'am," Scotty said, removing his hat.

"Chato tells me you are our mine foreman," Tashina said, going to the fireplace and pouring a cup of coffee.

"That's right ma'am," Scotty said, taking the steaming cup of coffee from Tashina and setting down on a chair made from a stump.

"Do you have much mining experience?"

"I have mined just about everything that can be mined. I brought fifteen miners with me on this trip. They are kind of rough but they are good men. Tomorrow I'll send the pack train back to town to bring in more supplies and tools. In two days another pack train should arrive that left town after us." Tashina was impressed with the big man. He knew exactly what needed to be done and was doing it. Finishing his coffee, Scotty asked, "Could you show me where the silver vein is so I will know what to have the pack train bring back?"

"Sure," Chato said. Leaving the cabin they walked up the ridge to the plateau where the silver was. Scotty saw the ore at once and went right to it. Taking the shovel lying next to the boulder he scraped the dirt away.

"It looks to be everything Sam said it was!" he exclaimed. Following the silver vein back into the ground, he stood up and looked around at the rockslide and the rocky peaks. "Some of this silver will be easy to get, and some we will have to work a little harder for." Turning to look at Tashina and Chato he said, "If that silver vein stays as strong as it looks, we will drive a shaft clear through the mountain if that's what it takes." Removing his hat he wiped the sweat from his brow. "In a month you won't recognize this place. We will mine this surface silver quickly and have a shaft started back into the mountain before the snows first begin to fall. We will probably have at least two pack trains constantly hauling supplies back and forth until we are through mining." Pointing to the side of the plateau he said, "Over there we will set up buildings to smelt the silver from the ore. Lumberjacks should arrive with the coming pack train to start cutting the timber for the structures and corrals we're going to need." Folding his arms across his chest, he looked slowly around at the pristine countryside. "I'm not sure what makes you the richer, taking this silver from the ground for wealth in dollars, or keeping the country the way it is for peace of mind?"

"What can we do to help you?" Chato asked, bringing Scotty back to the matter at hand.

"Nothing, nothing at all," Scotty replied dropping his arms. "I can take it from here."

Tashina smiled at the big man and said, "I hope you're hungry because I know I am."

"I'm starved!" Scotty exclaimed as Tashina turned and started down the mountain.

Supper that night was delicious elk steaks roasted slowly over the fire's hot coals. Tashina mixed up a batch of biscuits and baked them in a Dutch oven. As he drank his second cup of coffee, Scotty looked carefully around the cabin. He could tell these people lived a simple life by their meager possessions. *Being rich would change all of that for them*, he thought to himself. He watched Tashina as she tended to her cooking. She was one of the most beautiful Indian women he had ever seen. Chato looked Indian but with his fairer skin and green eyes, Scotty guessed his father was white. As Tashina brought several steaks over to the table Scotty asked her, "What happened to your husband if you don't mind my asking?"

The question startled Tashina. Chato started to reply when Tashina looked deep into his eyes and said, "He died when Chato was only a baby." Scotty knew he had touched a nerve and left it at that.

As he started wolfing down his steak, another question was bothering him so he asked it. "Why do you two live on this mountain alone? Surely you both crave the company of others?"

"Now that we have the mine, company shouldn't be a problem anymore," Chato told him chewing slowly on a piece of steak.

"Boy that's for sure! You're never going to be lonely on this mountain again," Scotty blurted.

"Who says we were lonely before?" Tashina said quietly as she sank her teeth into her bloody rare steak.

When supper was over, Scotty wiped his hands on his pants and thanked them for such a delicious meal. "The biscuits and steaks were perfect," he told Tashina. "Well, I guess I had better be going, it looks like its getting dark out." Standing, he thanked them again and then asks Tashina if she would walk with him for a ways down the mountain. Tashina looked at Chato and they both smiled.

Looking at Scotty she said, "That would be nice." Following him out the door she walked at his side.

Scotty looked up into the star-filled sky and said, "It's too bad the moon isn't full and casting its light down on us," in a gentle voice. "There is nothing prettier than a clear mountain sky, filled with bright stars and a large yellow moon."

Tashina laughed. "I love the moon too. It seems to let out the animal in me," she said in a teasing voice.

"Well I wish it were out in all its glory then," Scotty said, laughing with her.

Chato watched his mother walk away beside the big man and at first was amused. Then he became angry that Scotty wanted her to walk with him. As he stood next to the open cabin door his eyes turned fiery yellow and he turned into a demon wolf. With his wolf hearing, he could still hear them talking over a hundred yards away. It would be easy for him to kill Scotty, and he was tempted. But then who would supervise the mining? Uttering a terrible, deep growl, he snarled and slowly changed back to himself.

Tashina knew Chato would be angry and hoped he wouldn't turn into the wolf and destroy Scotty. They would need him to help save their people. "The reason I asked you to walk with me for a ways other than I think you are beautiful, is I wanted to tell you if you need anything at all let me know. Sam Jenkins will try to take this mine from you and your son. I have seen him do it before," he said in a serious voice. "If you get into any trouble at all let me know." Stopping, Tashina smiled up at him and thanked him for wanting to help. "Good night ma'am," he told her, tipping his hat as he continued walking back to his camp. As Tashina walked back to the cabin she was excited. Soon her people would be free!

In the weeks that followed it didn't take long for Scotty and his crew of miners to dig up all the surface silver and start blasting a shaft back into the mountainside. The mountain was a beehive of people constantly coming and going. A town had sprung up in the valley below, complete with several tent saloons and a brothel. A crew of laborers worked for weeks on the mountainside hacking and blasting a wagon road to the valley. When the rough road was done, wagonloads of supplies and equipment began to arrive. Prospectors scoured the mountain, searching for other possible silver strikes.

Howl of the Wolf

One morning three prospectors, each leading a donkey packed with supplies, hailed the cabin. Tashina had seen them come over the ridge and hoped they would go by without stopping.

"Hello in the cabin," an old-timer yelled. Opening the door Tashina walked outside to meet them. "Morning ma'am," the old-timer said, removing his hat.

"Good morning," Tashina answered.

"They say you folks are the owners of the mine up on the plateau and that you have lived here for many years," the old-timer said as he spat a stream of tobacco on the ground and wiped his shaggy gray beard off with his arm.

"Yes," Tashina replied. "Both my son and I were born in these mountains. Why do you ask?"

"I have mined in the mountain ranges around here the last thirty years but was always afraid to come into these mountains because of what the legend says," he exclaimed in a puzzled voice.

"What legend?" Tashina asked, starting to become irritated.

"The legend of a wolf tribe living high up on these mountains that turn into wolves at night during the full moon and kill and eat anyone who dare enter their country," the old man said as he studied the cabin and corrals.

"I am of the wolf tribe and the last of my people!" Tashina said with fire in her voice. "Do I look like a wolf to you?"

Feeling foolish, the man put his worn hat back on his head and said, "You're right, ma'am, I apologize for even bringing the subject up."

50

Tashina's eyes soften and she said in a kinder voice, "Legends will be legends."

"I guess you're right," he replied, still feeling foolish. "My partners here," he said, pointing to the two men standing behind him, "and I are going to strike out on our own to the back side of this mountain to see if we can get lucky and find a strike. Sorry we bothered you," he said as he walked away leading his donkey with his partners close behind.

Tashina smiled and said in a pleasant voice, "I hope you find what you are after," as they walked away up the mountain.

After they were out of hearing range of anyone who wasn't a wolf, one partner turned to look back at Tashina and said, "She is way too pretty to be a wolf, Abner. Are you sure that legend is right?"

"Shut up!" the old-timer said in a gruff voice. "If she is one, she can hear you!"

"Okay," the man replied, stumbling, as he looked back over his shoulder at Tashina who was still watching them. "But I still say she is way too pretty to be a wolf." Stopping and waiting for his partners to catch up, the old-timer waved at Tashina, who waved back.

"It's four days at least until another full moon and that should give us plenty of time to search this mountain for more silver. If we are lucky and find a strike, those silver bullets we cast will come in real handy," he whispered to them as they caught up. Tashina heard it all. Turning back to the cabin, she was surprised the old-timer believed the old legend. Later that night when Chato returned from helping Scotty at the mine she told him about her visitors.

The three miners camped that night at a small stream several ridges away from the cabin. Abner was busy cooking salt pork in a skillet while his partners Zeke and Dan were still scouring the hillside looking for signs of silver ore. Coffee was starting to boil in a pot next to the fire as Abner, using a leather glove, lifted the pot, poured a cup full, and set it down farther away from the flame. Taking a sip of the hot coffee he gingerly sat it down next to him and continued frying the pork. In a pot next to the hot coals he had beans slowly cooking. Looking up from his cooking he saw the donkeys still grazing below him. Just before dark, Zeke and Dan wandered back to the camp.

"Find anything worthwhile?" Abner asked as he dumped the skillet full of salt pork into the bean pot.

"Nothing but dirt and rocks," the two of them replied as they plopped down next to the fire. Zeke was tall and skinny as a beanpole. His face was long and covered with a scraggly blond beard. His coat was wool and well-worn as was his cotton shirt. A black leather belt made from old canvas held up his pants. His pant legs were tucked into the tops of black leather boots that had seen their better days. Dan was slightly younger than Zeke and much heavier. He was short and stocky and had a full reddish beard on his face. All three miners wore wide-brimmed hats that were all but worn out. Abner was much older than the other two and had the most experience. His scraggly beard was gray as was the hair left on the sides of his bald head. He had convinced them to come to this place, telling them no one had ever mined here before. "If the legends are true," he told them, "we have our silver bullets to protect us."

Abner wore a leather jacket over a cotton shirt tucked into wool pants. A wide leather belt fastened with a large brass buckle circled his small frame. They all wore leather boots with mule ear straps hanging loose at the sides. Dan wore canvas pants like Zeke and a soft leather shirt under a heavy wool coat. Dan used the leather glove to pick up the coffee pot and poured coffee into Zeke's cup while Zeke held it steady and then filled his own cup.

"After seeing that Indian woman back at the cabin this morning," Dan said setting the coffee pot down, "I think all that legend stuff is bunk! There is no way a woman like that could eat anyone," he stated in a serious voice.

Stirring the pot of beans with a large knife, Abner looked at him. "All I know is every Indian tribe and old timer I have ever known who knows of this place talks about the legend."

"I think we would be better off concentrating on finding our fortune in these mountains than worrying about the demon wolves of the legend," Zeke replied.

"You're probably right," Abner said in a quiet voice. "Grab your plates, boys, the beans are ready." After eating their fill of beans and salt pork they relaxed around the fire, smoking their pipes. Darkness was starting to blanket the mountainside when Abner got up, saying, "It's time to bring the asses in for the night."

"Wait!" Dan exclaimed, wide-eyed with a look of wonder on his face. Startled, Abner thought he must have heard something and looked down at Dan. Placing his hands under his pants Dan exclaimed, "My ass is already here, does that mean I don't have to get up?" Zeke and Dan both laughed out loud as Abner glared at Dan and went out to catch his ass. They were still laughing when they led their donkeys back to camp and tied them next to Abner's. Still giggling, they went to the fire and each got more coffee. Abner tried to act serious and mad, then broke down, and started laughing also.

"What a trio we make," he told them slapping himself on his knee. After smoking their pipes they turned in one by one, falling asleep as soon as they were under their blankets. The fire died down until it was only a soft red glow. The three donkeys were standing at the picket rope trying to sleep when one suddenly jerked its head up, startled by something. Listening with its pointy ears, all it could hear was the snoring of the three men next to the fire. Then it saw something moving in the shadows along the edge of the timber, only yards away. Turning to face the shadow it stomped its front foot and snorted. The other two donkeys were alert now and starting to become frightened. As the slight wind changed its direction the scent from the shadow drifted to them. Wide-eyed and frightened, they all snorted and stomped, tugging on the picket rope. Hearing the frightened donkeys, Abner sat up and grabbed his rifle.

"Zeke, Dan, are you awake?" he yelled in a half whisper.

"Yes," each replied.

"Something is out there and has frightened the asses." Out of the corner of his eye he saw the asses were calming down some, yet still alert. Suddenly, the quiet was broken by a howl just inside the timber and then another howl just below them on the open mountainside. Startled, both Zeke and Dan quickly sat up, rifles ready. Both men were visibly frightened as they heard another howl farther down the mountainside.

"Abner!" they yelled. "The wolves are all around us!"

Abner shook his head and told them, "It is only coyotes howling. What are you getting so worked up about?"

"Are you sure?" Dan asked, still scared.

"Sure, I'm sure," Abner replied. "When you hear a wolf howl it's like a rattlesnake's rattle, you will never forget it." Sheepishly, the two men returned to their blankets and lay back down. The rest of the night they listened to Abner's snoring, wondering if Abner was wrong.

Early the next morning after getting up they finished the leftover beans and salt pork for breakfast.

"Well, we made it through the night after all!" Abner smirked as he gobbled up his beans.

"That's not funny!" Dan replied in an irritated voice.

"Oh, relax," Abner said, smiling. "I told you if the legend is true, the demon wolves only run during the full moon. The moon won't be full for another couple of days. By then we will either be long gone or will be rich. If we stay, we need to be prepared, and that's why I gave each of you a silver bullet. If the legend is true, those silver bullets will be worth more than gold. If not we can pull the bullets and sell them in town."

"This whole thing about demon wolves gives me the creeps," Zeke told them both. "When we came through the mining camps we never heard anything about wolves attacking people in the full moon. I'm certain if the legend was true they would know about it by now, don't you think?" Abner and Dan looked at each other and then looked at Zeke.

"You're right," Dan said. "They have surely been here for a while and have had no trouble."

"Well, just in case, keep your silver bullets handy if we are still here during the full moon," Abner told them. They spent the rest of the morning looking hard for ore in one likely place after another. Abner took them high upon the mountain next to a tall rocky peak.

"Is that the peak you showed us from the bottom of the mountain that looks like a wolf's head just before dark?" Dan asked Abner.

"No, that peak is the one you can see over there," he said, pointing across the mountainside. "Just underneath that rocky peak is where the silver mine is." As they continued up the mountain, Abner said in an excited voice, "This is the best silver country we have been in so far." Looking up at the sun still high in the sky, he told them, "Spread out and use the rest of the day to comb the area thoroughly." As the afternoon sun slowly descended, the miners scoured the area hoping to find something. Zeke found a spot that looked promising but never found any hint of silver in the black ore he dug from the ground. Hailing the others, he called them over to where he was.

"This does look good!" Abner said as he saw where Zeke had been digging. Turning their donkeys loose to graze on the short grass, the three miners unlimbered their picks and shovels and started digging. It didn't take long for them to get winded. Stopping for a few minutes to rest, they wiped sweat off their foreheads, not speaking as they tried to catch their breath. And then they were at it again, the ringing of their shovels and picks striking the hard rock, echoing along the mountainside. Dan tore a chunk of ore from the ground with his pick and quickly bent down to examine it.

"Look!" he yelled as he broke the chunk apart with the end of the pick. Standing, he held up a fist-sized chunk of ore with tiny silver flakes sprinkled across it.

"Dan, that's silver!" Abner exclaimed, taking the big chunks of ore from Dan. Holding it up to see it better in the evening sunlight, he marveled at its beauty. "Look at all the silver specks in this chunk," he told the others in an excited voice. "It's not a vein but it may mean a vein is close by! Good job, partners! This spot really looks promising." Looking around him he said, "There isn't any good place with water and grass to camp at this high up, so we had better head down to that small creek we crossed earlier and camp there for the night." Catching their donkeys they hurried down the mountain and set up camp just as the sun disappeared under the mountaintop.

"What's for supper tonight?" Dan asked Abner after he put the donkeys out to graze for a while.

"Same as always, beans and more beans," Abner replied. "Where is Zeke?"

"He said he was going to see if he could get some fresh meat before dark, murmuring something about beans as he shouldered his rifle and went down the mountain."

"What's wrong with beans?" Abner asked as he stirred the simmering pot. "If what we found today pans out we may never have to eat beans again!"

"That's all right with me!" Dan replied, pouring a cup of coffee.

"I hope that fool doesn't waste his silver bullet on a deer or a rabbit," Abner said. "Don't even load your bullet until the night of the first full moon."

"That's what I plan on doing," Dan replied, taking his bullet from his pocket and turning it, watched it shine in the firelight.

Zeke was tired of beans every night and hoped he could find some fresh meat for supper before it got dark. They had been so busy looking for silver the last couple of days they hadn't taken the time to do any hunting. He walked down the mountain along the creek until he came upon a grassy meadow. *This would be a good place to shoot a deer coming out to feed before dark*, he thought to himself. Sitting on a stump at the timber's edge, he waited, rifle ready. The sun was down now and there was only about fifteen minutes until dark. The light began fading fast as he squinted his eyes to see. *It was going to be dark tonight*, he thought as he looked at the cloudy overcast sky. Suddenly at the lower end of the meadow a deer stood at the timber's edge. It was really getting dark quick and all he could make out was the outline of the deer as it loped out to the middle of the meadow. Bringing his rifle up he watched the deer run and knew it wasn't a deer because of the way it loped instead of ran. He could barely see the figure as he sighted down his rifle. The figure suddenly stood on its hind legs like a bear. "It's a bear!" he muttered to himself, cocking his rifle. Suddenly the blur raised its head and howled a deep, blood-curdling howl. Startled, Zeke fired before he was ready. The recoil knocked Zeke back momentarily. Levering another cartridge into his rifle, he turned to run when the creature grabbed him by his shoulders and shook him so hard he dropped his rifle. Yelling in pain he tried to get free as the creature picked him up high in the air, growling savagely. Zeke twisted his body and looked into the yellow eyes of a hideous wolf creature. He tried to scream but was so frightened he couldn't speak. *The legend is true!* his mind screamed as the wolf tore at his chest with its terrible teeth. The pain was unbearable as Zeke screamed and then was gone.

"Zeke better hurry with the fresh game or supper will be over," Abner remarked stirring the beans again.

"What was that?" Dan asked looking in the direction Zeke had gone.

"It sounded like a howl and a rifle shot," Abner answered. "I hope he doesn't drag a dead coyote back to camp and expect to use it for camp meat. We will wait a few minutes more but as soon as these beans are ready, I'm going to eat." When the beans were ready, Abner filled his plate and started to eat. "I almost wish Zeke had brought in a coyote for supper. Any fresh meat would be better than these beans," exclaimed Abner. Dan got his plate and heaped it full of the steaming beans.

"He better hurry back if he knows what's good for him or he will miss out on this excellent supper," Dan said as both men laughed. They were engrossed in gulping down their supper when a terrible wolf howl pierced the silence of the night. Both men almost choked as they threw their plates high in the air and scrambled for their rifles.

"Wolf!" Abner screamed, clearing the beans from his mouth. Finding his rifle he fumbled for the silver bullet deep in his pocket. Hearing a savage growl, he looked up to see the yellow eyes of a hideous creature standing above him. In blind panic he tried to lift his rifle as the snarling demon tore the rifle from his trembling hands and savagely ripped open his throat. Blood was spurting everywhere as the wolf dropped his body and looked at Dan who was trying desperately to load his silver bullet in his rifle. Dan saw the demon kill his friend, blood squirting everywhere and was so frightened his fingers wouldn't work anymore. Fumbling with the bullet, he dropped it on the ground as the wolf fed on Abner's raw flesh, growling at him. Summoning all his strength and willpower Dan dropped his rifle and ran screaming into the darkness. Tripping over a stump, he fell headfirst into the dirt. Blindly scrambling to his knees he looked back towards the fire and saw the wolf tearing a huge chunk of meat from Abner's body and gulp it down. Screaming, he struggled to its feet and ran headlong down the mountainside. Branches slapped him in the face and tore at his clothes as he ran through the timber. He was exhausted and ready to collapse when he tripped over something and rolled headlong into a small meadow. Getting to his hands and knees he found a rifle lying in the grass. Picking up the rifle he knew it was Zeke's.

"Zeke!" he yelled. "Are you okay?" Scanning the darkness he looked quickly for his friend. "Zeke, can you hear me?" he whispered. Remembering the wolf, he turned to run again and stumbled, his foot striking something on the ground. "Zeke is that you?" he asked, bending down to see what it was. Reaching down he felt something wet and sticky. "Zeke is that you?" he muttered, turning the object over. It was then that he saw the object he was holding was his partially-eaten friend, covered in blood. "No!" Dan screamed as he jumped up and ran down the mountain. Frantically he ran until his lungs were bursting and then fell to his hands and knees trying desperately to catch his breath. Sitting up, he leaned against a tree trunk and watched the trail, trembling violently. He was starting to hope he had escaped the terror when he heard the wolf howl. His heart skipped a beat and he started shaking uncontrollably. Too exhausted to move he saw the fiery yellow eyes of the wolf. It was running straight towards him, snarling and growling loudly. Closing his eyes he felt the demon grab him savagely and then felt his life's blood being drained from his body as everything went black.

At daybreak the next morning, Tashina took the coffee pot from the fireplace, and going outside, dumped out the old coffee grounds. The morning was cool and she could just see her breath in the early morning light. Going to the stream, she washed out the pot and then filled it with fresh water. Chato was gone last night and she knew when he returned this morning he would like hot coffee to help wash down all the bloody feasting from the night before. With the coffee pot full, she started to stand and felt the presence of someone standing behind her.

"Good morning mother," she heard her son say as she turned to face him.

"How did it go last night?" She asked him with a wicked smile on her face.

"You were right, waiting until the second night really caught them off guard."

"Where were they?"

"Under that far peak," Chato told her pointing back behind him. "They each carried one of these," he said in a serious voice, holding out three silver bullets. "They foolishly had them in their pockets instead of their rifles, although it wouldn't have mattered much." Taking the bullets, Tashina turned them in her hand remembering the silver musket ball Jack had years ago.

"I saw my father die after being shot in the heart with a ball of silver," she said in a sad voice. "Those miners came prepared and heeded the warnings of the legend. The only thing they didn't prepare for is you," she said smiling at her son. "Only you could have destroyed them without the full moon! Now wash up good and come inside for some hot coffee and rest. I'm going to fix some breakfast and I suppose you are not hungry anymore, are you?" Smiling, Chato shook his head slowly. Walking back to the cabin, Tashina could smell the blood on Chato and felt the wolf inside her growl, eager for the full moon.

Moon of Terror

The morning of the full moon came quickly and as Tashina cooked breakfast she listened to Chato tell her how well the mining was progressing. "Scotty says they are digging into the mountainside about ten feet per day now. They are already several hundred feet deep."

"How much longer until they break into the cave?" Tashina asked, filling her coffee cup and sitting at the table.

"I'm not sure, it all depends on where exactly and how deep the cave is."

"I hope we are not too late!" she said, staring at the cup of steaming coffee. "I haven't heard the howling of my people for many years."

"Nor have I," Chato replied, seeing the worry on his mother's face. "But we both know we can only be killed by silver penetrating our hearts and that has to mean at least some of them are still alive." Toying with her coffee cup, Tashina looked at him teary-eyed and nodded her head. "Be careful tonight, mother, we don't know how many others know about the legend and are packing weapons loaded with silver bullets."

Smiling at him, Tashina wiped the tears from her eyes and said, "I'm always careful, but it's getting harder and harder to keep the wolf in me away from the miners camps and all those people."

"Soon," Chato said, his eyes turning fiery yellow, "we will break into the cave and our people will glut themselves until there is no more blood and flesh left on this mountain!"

Late that evening as the sun dropped behind the mountains, Ben Thunder quickly loaded the deer he had shot on his saddle horse and lashed it on. He was a meat hunter for the mining camp and was finding it harder and harder to find enough game to keep the camp supplied. He had ridden several miles from the camp and hunted all day before he spooked this deer from the timber and shot it. As darkness started to fall, he was thankful for the full moon glowing in the night sky. In the bright moonlight he would be able to make his way back to camp, leading his horse. It would take most of the night to walk back and butcher the deer, but he knew fresh meat for the miner's breakfast would be worth it to him. He was a tall man with wide shoulders and strong arms. He wore a fringed buckskin jacket over a soft buckskin hunting shirt. A wide belt around his waist carried his large bowie knife and scabbard as well as cartridge loops full of rifle cartridges. His pants were leather and hung down to the tops of his beaded moccasins. Gray hair hung to his shoulders and matched his drooping gray mustache. A hat made from bear's fur was pressed firmly down on his head. Blue eyes watched everything from behind his beak like nose and high cheekbones. He had lived as a trapper most of his life until beaver became worthless. For several years, he became a buffalo hunter following the great herds, slaughtering the buffalo for their hides and tongues. Disgusted with the slaughter of buffalo, he turned to hunting meat for the mining camps. It paid better and let him do the things he liked to do.

Finished loading the deer, he removed his pipe and filled it full of fresh tobacco. Gazing into the sky, he lit his pipe and inhaled the strong tobacco smoke. The moonlight caressed the mountainside, allowing Ben to see his shadow as he grabbed his bridle reins and started his long walk. Ben tried to stay at the edge of the timber or out in the open as much as possible. In the timber it was pitch black with hardly any moonlight getting through the tops of the tall pines. Gripping his pipe tightly in his teeth, he looked at the moon and chuckled out loud. He knew the legend of this country and thought it was just a clever way to keep people away from the silver. Apparently not many people knew of it, or remembered, or there would be silver bullets everywhere.

"What a pure waste of good silver," he muttered in disgust, removing his pipe from his teeth. "My God, what children people are to believe in such nonsense," he said out loud, startling his pony. "Whoa, boy, take it easy, it's only me talking to myself again." Tugging on the reins he continued walking towards the mining camps.

"People who turn into wolves during the full moon and eat people. How could anyone believe such garbage?" Any trouble he had run into had always been taken care of with lead and if that weren't enough the sting of his bowie knife would finish the job. Stopping at the timber's edge, he knocked the ashes from his pipe and put it away. Wolves, he had seen plenty of wolves hunting buffalo and they never gave him any trouble so he never figured the legend of this mountain would either. Entering the timber he carefully picked his way through the dark forest floor. He was making good time and only had several more ridges to go to get back to the camps.

Suddenly, Ben stopped with his rifle ready. The hairs on the back of his neck were standing up the way they had many times before, warning him of danger. Levering a cartridge into his rifle, he strained to see into the black timber surrounding him. His horse jerked its head up, snorting and pulling against the bridle reins. "Whoa, boy," he whispered, turning to calm the pony as it jerked back again. Wide-eyed, nostrils flared, it tore the bridle reins from his hand. "Whoa!" he said louder, trying to grab the reins as the frightened horse turned and bolted away. He could hear the horse tearing through the timber as he quickly turned to face whatever was out there. He was calm as he stood waiting for the next move. Hearing a twig snap to his side he turned to see two fiery yellow eyes glaring at him. Immediately he fired at the eyes and then levered another cartridge into his rifle. Ben heard the bullet strike something and a deep growl at the same time. The eyes disappeared and then flashed through the timber circling him. Quickly he fired shot after shot, hitting branches and trees as he spun around, firing at the creature. When his rifle clicked on an empty chamber he threw the rifle down and drew his bowie knife.

"Come on then!" he challenged, still not knowing what to expect. A terrible howl erupted in the timber right next to him and fear swept through his body like a shock wave causing him to almost fall to his knees. Remembering the legend, he knew his rifle would be useless. "It's true! He muttered out loud, "It's true!" Holding his knife, ready to cut and slash, he started backing up slowly. After traveling twenty yards he stopped, sensing something behind him. Freezing, he listened hard to determine where it was. Hearing a deep growl, he spun around, slashing wickedly with his knife. As he turned he saw terrible yellow eyes as strong jaws bit his hand holding the knife off at the wrist. Grabbing his bloody stub, he screamed and ran as fast as he could from the demon. The pain was almost unbearable as he stumbled through the dark timber, branches tearing at his face and clothing.

It was a wolf! His mind screamed as he ran. Warm blood was pumping through the fingers of his good hand as he tried to stop the bleeding. He was getting very weak now and had lost too much blood. He must stop and tie off his arm before he passed out and bled to death. Feeling very dizzy he fell to his knees and then to his side. Tearing a fringe from his jacket, he wrapped it around his stub and tied it off. With the blood flow stopped, he tried to get to his feet but was too weak and dizzy. Falling back on his side he gasped for breath unable to breathe. Feeling the world spinning around him, the pain was suddenly gone. As things stopped spinning, he saw the yellow eyes and hideous form of the demon wolf standing on its hind legs above him. He saw the wolf raise its head and emit a chilling howl. He wasn't scared anymore and felt peaceful as the wolf started to feed on him.

Tashina bathed herself at the creek the next morning as the sun started to lighten the horizon. She had had only fed once last night, trying to take the wolf far from the camps. She shivered as she washed the blood from her body. Once she had bathed, she went to the cabin and put on a clean dress. The cabin was toasty warm when she entered and soon the goose bumps on her skin went away. Chato saw her come in, smiled, and turned over under his blankets and went back to sleep. Tashina filled the coffee pot from the stream and soon had hot coffee brewing on the fire. Smelling the coffee, Chato got up and poured himself a cup.

"Did you stay here all night?" Tashina asked.

"Yep," he answered, sipping the hot coffee. "In order to keep our secret hidden, it's important to have one of us here while the other hunts. Did anyone see you come back this morning?"

"If they did, all they saw was a woman bathing in the dim light of the early dawn," she replied, laughing out loud. Chato got up and started to go outside. "'Where are you going?" she asked in a puzzled voice.

"Some of us still haven't eaten yet," he said. "I hope I can carve a few more steaks off of that elk carcass hanging in the trees. Would you like a steak?" he turned and asked her. Indicating with her tiny hands over her stomach that she was stuffed she shook her head, laughing wickedly.

Tashina slept the rest of the day, knowing the wolf in her would run again when darkness came. Chato visited Scotty at the mine and was delighted with how well it was going. He was sure the shaft back into the side of the mountain was getting close to breaking into the ancient cave.

"If the weather continues to hold," Scotty told him, "we should be almost to the middle of the mountain in a week's time or less. Sam should be here in a week to pay you your share of the mine's profits."

"How do you know that?" Chato asked.

"He sent a letter with the last pack train, telling me so. Make sure he gives you receipts of the total weight of silver mined so far. Be careful, like I told your mother, he will take you if he can." Chato spent most of the day helping Scotty, knowing his mother was resting in the cabin.

"How about you and your mother joining me for supper tonight?" Scotty asked late that afternoon.

"I would love to," Chato replied. "But Tashina has been feeling sick and probably won't be able to join us," he said, pretending to be worried.

"Tell her I hope she starts feeling better," Scotty replied.

"I will," Chato said walking back to the cabin.

"Meet me at my bunk later and we will go get two of the largest steaks we can find!" Scotty yelled. When Chato got back to the cabin Tashina was already up, sitting next to the fire. He could smell the wolf in her, aching to come out.

"Scotty invited us to dinner tonight. I told him you were feeling poorly and probably couldn't make it."

"That's an understatement," Tashina said, feeling the wolf growling in her stomach. Chato changed his shirt and tucking the shirttail into his pants, he turned to Tashina.

"Good hunting," he said, pulling his hat down tightly on his head.

"Enjoy your steak!" she smirked, laughing at him as he left the cabin. Chato pulled the collar up on his leather jacket, shielding his neck from the chilly breeze. The sun was almost down now and he could already see the moon peeking over the horizon. Hands in his pockets, he walked quickly up the ridge and down to the miner's camp below. Scotty's bunk was in a large tent house at the upper end of the camp, so he never had far to go. He could hear a piano playing somewhere in the center of the camp and a mule braying in the far corrals. The whole town was lit up with lamplights, giving it an eerie glow. Walking quickly to Scotty's tent, he opened the flap and walked inside. There were at least a dozen bunks in the long tent, each piled high with bedding and in some cases miners already trying to get some sleep. Scotty's bunk was at the end of the tent next to the wall. He saw Scotty combing his hair using a piece of broken mirror and an old comb.

Scotty saw him walking up and dropping the comb and mirror in an open trunk under his bunk he asked, "Well, how do I look?" "Don't answer that honestly or you will hurt my feelings," he quickly replied. Taking his derby hat from the bunk, he placed it carefully on his combed hair. "Well, I guess I'm as ready as I can be," he said, slapping Chato on the back. "Are you hungry my friend?"

"Starved," Chato replied following him out of the tent.

"I know a place that serves up huge beefsteaks any way you want them," he said, leading Chato through the camp. The piano noise was getting closer all the time as they wound their way down the narrow street.

"Smell that?" Scotty said as they rounded a large tent with wood sides. "This is the place!" he exclaimed walking through the open doorway. Chato could see eight round tables with chairs all around them, crammed into the limited space in the tent. Lamps were hung down the middle of the large tent and lighted it well. Chato could smell steaks cooking and the tobacco smoke that hung like a cloud at the crest of the tent. The place was almost packed but Scotty bulled his way between the chairs and found an empty table next to the far wall. Several of the miners recognized Chato and greeted him as he walked by. Everyone knew Scotty and teased him, saying the steaks were all gone and he might as well go back to his bunk. Scotty raised his big hand and waved them away, saying the good steaks were all saved just for him and never given to the likes of them. Laughing, everyone went back to enjoying their dinners. A short, round man in an apron walked up to their table and, seeing Scotty, greeted him warmly.

"I know what you want, but what about your friend here?" the man exclaimed, a short cigar held tightly in his teeth.

"Danny this is Chato, he is one of the owners of this silver mine." Wiping his hand on his apron Danny reached out and shook Chato's hand.

"Glad to meet you," he said between his clenched teeth.

"Good to meet you," Chato replied.

"How do you want your steak cooked?" Danny asked.

"Make mine thick and bloody rare," Chato replied.

"Bring us a couple mugs of cold beer," Scotty told him.

"Coming right up," Danny said going to the back of the tent. It wasn't long before he returned with two large mugs of strong beer with foam an inch thick covering the top of the mugs. Scotty raised his mug in his huge paw and took several large swallows before setting it back on the table. Chato enjoyed the taste of the lather and the cool bite of the strong beer as he lifted his mug and took several swallows.

"Man that tastes good at the end of the day!" Scotty exclaimed. Chato agreed as they each took another drink. It wasn't long before Danny returned carrying a large plate, completely covered by thick steak.

"Here is your steak," he said to Chato sitting it on the table.

"That never took long," Chato said in a surprised voice.

"It didn't take long to cook a steak bloody rare," Danny chuckled as he turned to Scotty. "Yours should be ready in a few more minutes."

"I hope so, my stomach is starting to eat me on the inside." Laughing Danny left the table. "How is it?" Scotty asked Chato as he sliced off a piece and spearing it with his fork popped it into his mouth.

"Mmmm ... delicious," Chato replied. *It was really good*, he thought as he sliced off another piece. By the time Danny brought Scotty's steak, he had already eaten half of his. Danny also brought two large baked potatoes and set them on the table with a tub of butter.

"How about a couple more beers?" Scotty said. Danny returned with a pitcher of beer and sat it on the table. "That is more like it," Scotty exclaimed, chewing on a mouthful of steak. Chato ate his steak and baked potato slowly, enjoying his meal. He liked Scotty and would be sorry to see him die if it came to that. Once Scotty got his steak, he never talked much. He was hungry and enjoyed every bite. Both men finished their steaks and potatoes at the same time, and washing them down with another mug of beer, leaned back in their chairs to relax. Danny returned with two large cigars and left a candle in a dish for them to light them with. Chato had never had a cigar before and after lighting it, quickly found it better than his pipe.

"I am stuffed!" Scotty said in agony as he smoked his cigar. Chato nodded in agreement and then heard a miner in the street outside yell out Scotty's name.

Killer Bear

"What now?" Scotty muttered as he pushed his chair back and stood up. Motioning to Danny he threw several coins on the table and then went outside with Chato close behind. "What is it?" he said in a loud voice to the waiting miner.

"You better come and see for yourself!" the miner exclaimed in a frightened voice. Carrying a lamp, the miner led them through the camp and out to the far side of the large corrals. Scotty could see the mules and horses all bunched up and knew that something had frightened them. Chato knew what it was the minute they left the dining tent. He could smell blood and the wolf his mother had become. In the moonlight he could see a crowd of people gathered around something. As the miner got closer with the lamp, Scotty took it and waded into the crowd.

"Get back!" he growled as he tried to see what the problem was. As the crowd moved back he saw a sickening sight. The body of what used to be a man lay mangled before him. Blood was everywhere and the body was almost unrecognizable, with large portions of flesh missing. "My God!" Scotty exclaimed in disgust. "What could have done this?"

"It must have been a bear!" a miner exclaimed.

"Yes, that must be what did this terrible thing," Scotty said, looking at the bloody clothes torn to shreds all over the ground. "Some of you guys get a blanket and cover what is left of this poor man. We will bury him in the morning before we hunt this killer bear down and kill it." Turning he looked at Chato and asked, "Have you ever seen anything like this up here before?"

Chato pretended to be shocked. "Nothing this terrible has ever happened here before." Scotty gave orders for armed men to guard the corrals in case the bear returned wanting more meat and told everybody else to get some sleep.

"We still need to keep mining tomorrow," he told them. "We will send several of our best hunters and trackers after this killer!" As Scotty turned to go, Chato thanked him for the wonderful supper.

"I expect I'd better be heading home and check on Tashina."

"Be careful and tell your mother I hope she starts feeling better." Remembering Chato was not armed he asked if he wanted to borrow a rifle for his walk home.

"No," Chato said. "I think all this excitement probably scared the bear away for awhile."

"You're probably right," Scotty replied, watching his friend walk away in the moonlight. Chato left the miners and walked at a steady pace back up the ridge and down to the cabin. The cabin was dark when he got there, as he knew it would be. His mother would not return until morning, when the wolf in her left. He hoped if she continued to hunt tonight she would take the wolf farther away. With the whole camp in an uproar finding the badly-eaten body, they would need to be extra careful. Starting a fire in the fireplace, he soon had the cabin warm enough to take his jacket off.

Just before dawn the next morning Chato heard the cabin door open and saw his mother enter. "Are you okay?" he asked sitting up.

"I'm fine," she said, smiling.

"How many times did you feed last night?" he asked, getting up to put more wood in the fireplace.

"Only once, I roamed farther away but couldn't find anything," Tashina replied.

"I was with the miners when they found your kill last night." Getting the coffee pot, he opened the cabin door and went to the stream to fill it full of fresh water. The sun was rising over the mountaintop, its rays of sunshine falling across the mountainside. Chato could see miners going to work, carrying their lunches up the mountain. Hearing riders, he turned and saw four riders starting down the ridge towards the cabin. He could see Scotty waving at him as they approached.

"Morning," Scotty said in a deep voice as they rode up.

"Good morning," Chato replied. "You're out bright and early this morning." Chato looked at the others with Scotty and guess they must be hunters out to kill the bear. The three riders were all dressed in buckskins and looked rough as the outdoors. "With those gentlemen behind you, I would guess you were going after the bear," Chato said, smiling, watching the men behind Scotty.

"Right you are," Scotty replied. "The sooner we can get the bastard the quicker we can all go back to our business. These men behind me are the best trackers and hunters in the camp," Scotty told him. "One of their comrades and maybe the best tracker of them all has not showed up for two days. The chances are the bear got him. How is your mother doing?" Scotty asked.

"She is still kind of under the weather," Chato said in a sad voice. The door of the cabin opened and Tashina stepped out, waving to Scotty. "I figured you would try to find the bears tracks where the killing took place," Chato told them.

"We searched around the kill site pretty good before we left but couldn't find any bear sign," a rough-looking hunter said as he spat a stream of tobacco in the dirt. "We did find some large tracks that resembled a wolf's in the timber above the killings." Chato shielded his eyes with his hand from the sun now on top of the horizon.

"I thought we would ride up here and see if you wanted to accompany these hunters," Scotty exclaimed. "You know this mountain country better than anyone."

"I'm not a very good tracker," Chato told him.

"Don't worry about that," a buckskin-clad hunter said. "We will do the tracking." Chato thought about it for a moment and then told them he needed to stay at the cabin while his mother was sick.

"Besides, I would just get in the way. There is nothing about this mountain that I know that these experienced hunters couldn't figure out in a few minutes." Holding up the pot of fresh water, he told them they were welcome to stay for hot coffee as soon as he got it brewed.

"We had better be getting along," Scotty said, declining. "I need to go to the mine and make sure everything is okay."

"And we need to find us a killer bear and an old friend!" the tobacco-chewing hunter said, spitting another stream of tobacco in the dirt.

Turning their ponies away from Chato, the hunters rode away. Sitting on his horse Scotty watched the three hunters ride off.

"Those boys are rough," he said in a serious tone. "If anyone can kill the bear they can. Well, I better be getting to the mine," Scotty said, waving goodbye to Chato as he rode away. As he rode past the cabin, Tashina stepped out of the door and began coughing as she waved at him.

"Good morning ma'am," Scotty said, removing his hat.

"Good morning Scotty," Tashina replied between coughs. "What's all the commotion about?"

"Nothing for you to worry your pretty head about," he told her in a flustered voice. "Now would you please go back inside before you catch your death of pneumonia?" Still coughing, Tashina nodded her head and went back inside. Putting his hat back on his head and waving at Chato, Scotty rode away. Following Tashina into the cabin, Chato shut the door behind them.

"What did they want?" Tashina asked, no longer coughing.

"A bear killed a miner at the camp corrals last night," he said putting fresh coffee grounds in the pot and setting it over the fire. "They're going to track it and kill it before it hurts anyone else. Also, one of their experienced hunters has been missing for several days. You don't know anything about those tragedies do you?" he said with a laugh.

"No, nothing at all, how could I, when I have been sick the last couple days?" she said, coughing again. Both of them laughed sinister laughs and then Chato stopped and looked very serious.

"They talked about large wolf tracks they found above the corrals. We both need to be very careful from now on. We mustn't disrupt the mining now, when we are so close to freeing our people."

"You're right. I must control the wolf in me, and stay away, but with so many people on the mountain now it's very hard. When I'm wolf all I want is blood and flesh and the camps are the easiest places to find it."

"We are lucky this time that Scotty is going to work in the mines and not shut them down until the danger has passed."

"How much longer until they break into the cave?" Tashina asked in a weary voice.

"Soon, very soon," Chato said, starting to become excited. "Soon we will run in packs and kill everything still left on the mountain!" he snarled, his eyes starting to turn yellow.

Each night after the bear attacks Tashina took the wolf far from the camps. She found less and less to feed on and the hunger in her was tremendous, and she knew she wouldn't be able to control wolf any longer.

The hunters hadn't found any bear tracks but did manage to find the bones and bloody clothes of their fellow hunter. At one point they found bear tracks but they were leaving the area fast. The tracks were from a young bear, not something able to kill and eat a grown man. Wolf tracks were found everywhere, even near their fallen comrade's bones. The tracks were strange—they were large and looked almost like the balls of the human foot in places.

Scotty stopped by the cabin to visit with Tashina and Chato several days after bringing the hunters by. "They searched for several days for whatever might have killed the miner and their comrade, but found nothing," Scotty told Tashina and Chato as he sat in the cabin and drank a cup of coffee. "The whole camp is in an uproar, scared the bear—or whatever it is—might return." Smiling at Tashina he told her, "It's sure nice to see you are feeling better."

"Thanks, Scotty, I'm feeling a little better every day now."

"Sam should be here any day now and that will help. Maybe he can console everyone, while I focus my attention back on the mine."

"I hope he gets here soon!" Chato exclaimed. "I can't wait to see how rich we have become!"

"Maybe then we can hire our own bear killers," Tashina replied, laughing out loud.

"Money can buy almost anything," Scotty stated, smiling at Tashina. "Well, I just wanted to come by this morning to let you both know what's been going on and to see how you are feeling," he said, looking tenderly at Tashina.

"Thanks, Scotty," they both said, following him out the door.

"Remember when Sam comes, have him show you proof of what he pays you for," he told them, mounting his horse.

"How is the mining coming?" Tashina asked.

"We have followed the silver vein almost halfway into the mountain now. It's not as wide as it was but it seems to still be going strong."

"I'll come see if I can lend a hand later," Chato told him as Scotty rode off towards the mine, waving at Tashina.

"That man is in love with you!" Chato said, grinning at Tashina.

"Oh, you're exaggerating!" Tashina replied, blushing a little. Watching him ride away she told Chato, "Scotty is one of the few friends we have, we would be wise to cherish him." Tashina felt tired and hungry as she entered the cabin and sat at the table.

"Hang in there," Chato told her, placing his hand on her arm. "Only one more night of the full moon and you can relax for a while." Nodding her head Tashina knew tonight she wouldn't be able to control the wolf.

Escape of the Damned

As the late afternoon sun slowly inched its way towards the horizon, the sound of axes biting deep into pine logs echoed across the mountainside. Sinking his ax deep into the top of the tree stump, the logger yelled down to the others. "It's time to get what we have ready and finish loading the wagon." The four men below him were busy trimming branches from several felled trees. Stopping, they sank their axes into the downed trees and went to the wagon. It was a lumber wagon with a large, heavy, flat bed and cut poles stuck into the sides to keep logs from rolling off.

"If we're going to get this load back by dark we better get moving," the first logger told them as he met them at the wagon. He was a tall man with long, lean muscles, dressed in a heavy wool shirt and wool pants that were tucked into the tops of his lace up leather boots. Wide suspenders went over his shoulders and hooked to the front of his pants. A wide leather belt was buckled around his waist with a large knife and scabbard hanging from it. His sleeves were rolled up, showing red underwear underneath. A cap made from wool sat on his short brown hair. His face was thin with high cheekbones and the narrow chin. His eyes were green and large, looking out from behind a face covered with whisker stubble. Trevor was his name and he was the foreman of this crew of loggers. They were cutting logs to be used at the miner's camps just over the hill.

"Well, let's load up and get out of here!" a man of medium build and height said in a raspy voice. "I know they never found the bear," he said looking all around, "but the stories about wolves on this mountain make me nervous."

"Oh, they are just tales to scare people away from the mining," a heavyset young man with peach fuzz on his face replied with a chuckle. He was of medium height with wide shoulders and was stocky with a wide thick chest and big arms and legs.

"That may be what you say now, Tommy, but you will sing a different tune it the wolf sets its sights on you," the man rasped in his weak voice.

"We will all get a chance to see what lurks on this side of this mountain in the dark if we don't get this wagon loaded," Trevor said in a deep voice. Working together they loaded the wagon full of the logs they had cut that day. Once loaded, they put up the side poles and lashed the logs on with a large rope.

"It's quitting time boys!" the man with a raspy voice said, running to climb up on the wagon seat next to the driver. Trevor watched the wagon lumber away, realizing only he and Tommy and were still there.

"You had better catch up with them, Tommy."

"What are you going to do?" Tommy asked.

"I need to un-harness, grain, and put up our skid horse. Besides, there is still at least another hour before dark," he said looking at the sun looming over the mountaintops.

"Let me put up the skid horse and feed him," Tommy said, going to the horse and leading him towards the corral.

"Well, if you insist," Trevor said. "While you are doing that I may as well trim a few more limbs off those logs so we can load them in the morning." Walking back up the ridge he pulled his ax free and continued knocking branches off the logs. Quickly finishing that chore, he decided to start chopping the logs to length while he waited for Tommy to finish. It wasn't long before the ringing of the ax could be heard at a feverish pace. Tommy finished with the horse and saw Trevor was chopping logs to length now. Looking at the sun beginning to disappear under the mountaintop he decided to saddle Trevor's horse for him. Trevor always stayed late and got things ready for the next day. After saddling Trevor's horse, Tommy walked up the ridge to where Trevor was busy chopping, unaware of anything around him.

He kept thinking, *I'll just chop one more in half and then I'll quit, and then just one more.* He was glad Tommy reminded him it was time to go. Sinking the blade of the ax in the stump again, he wiped the sweat from his brow.

"It is getting kind of late," Tommy said, a little worry in his voice. "I saddled your horse for you."

"Thanks, Tommy," he said as he looked at the mountaintop and saw the sun was already down. Darkness was starting to fall across the mountainside. "Well, at least the moon is still full," he said pointing at the big yellow moon, high in the sky. Seeing the worry on Tommy's face he said, "Don't worry, Tommy, I haven't left until after dark all this week. There is nothing to worry about, if the bear was here, it is long gone now with all the people hunting it." Tommy looked down across the mountainside and saw it was almost dark. *Trevor was right,* he thought to himself, *the moon would help light up their way back to camp.* Turning to walk down the ridge to the horse, both men were startled by terrible howl just over the ridge from where they were.

"What was that?" Tommy whispered in a frightened voice.

"It sounded like a wolf!" Trevor said. "Go to the horse and get my rifle, maybe we can put an end to this wolf problem once and for all." "Hurry!" he told Tommy. "Get it and meet me at the top of the ridge. I'm going to take a quick peek over the ridge and see if it's still there." As Tommy scrambled down the ridge in the dark, Trevor slowly worked his way to the top and looked over. Reaching the horse, Tommy quickly pulled the rifle from the saddle scabbard and rushed back up the ridge. Gasping for breath he saw Trevor signal for him to get down and be quiet. Rushing to Trevor's side, he handed him the rifle. Trevor levered a cartridge into the chamber and then sat very still. A howl broke the silence again, this time very close. Trevor was startled by the howl and almost dropped his rifle. Tommy was terrified and was ready to run except Trevor grabbed him by his arm, holding him there. The top of the ridge was open except for several trees. In the moonlight, Trevor should be able to see what was howling, but he couldn't. Then he saw the shadow of what looked like a frightened deer run out into the open. It was followed by a loping shadow that quickly caught the deer and brought it to the ground. They could hear growling and the frantic bleating sound of the deer before it died.

"It's a wolf!" Trevor told Tommy, "feeding on a deer." There was a slight breeze blowing into Trevor's eyes making them water and strain even more to make out the wolf in the moonlight. Suddenly the breeze changed and came from behind Trevor and Tommy and out across the ridge top. Trevor watched the wolf suddenly sit up from its prey and look right at him. Its eyes were fiery yellow, unlike any eyes he had seen before. Then in shock he saw the wolf stand upright on its hind legs.

"Oh my God!" Tommy exclaimed as the wolf stood up. Quickly Trevor brought his rifle up and aiming at the creature before him, fired. He saw the wolf get knocked sideways slightly and then dropping to all fours, it started running straight at them, its yellow eyes burning. Firing three more quick shots, Trevor yelled for Tommy to run, but Tommy was already gone. Seeing the bullets hit the wolf with little or no effect, Trevor turned and ran down the ridge. Halfway down the ridge, he saw Tommy sprawled out on the ground. Dazed, Tommy got up with Trevor's help.

"I tripped," Tommy said getting to its feet. Hearing a terrible growl Trevor looked up to see the wolf almost on top of them.

"Run Tommy!" he screamed, pushing Tommy down the ridge as he lifted his rifle. He almost had the wolf in his sights when with a horrible growl it ran headlong into him, knocking him sprawling. The rifle went off, startling the wolf creature as it clattered down the ridge. Seeing Tommy, the wolf took too long leaps and pulled him to the ground. Tommy was screaming madly when Trevor got to his feet. He was shaken but unhurt. Seeing the wolf bite at Tommy's back savagely, he drew his knife and threw it into the wolf's broad back. As the long blade buried itself into the wolf's back, it howled in pain and rage. Reaching back with humanlike hands it pulled the knife free. In a rage it growled savagely and ran back it up the ridge towards Trevor.

"Run, Tommy, run!" Trevor screamed as he tried to run away from the wolf. Tommy looked up to see the demon chase after Trevor and quickly got to his feet and ran down the ridge.

"Run, Tommy!" He heard Trevor scream as the wolf jumped on him, tearing at him savagely. Tommy reached the already frightened horse and could tell he was bleeding badly. Trying to calm the horse he quickly found the stirrup and mounted. He could hear Trevor screaming as he kicked the horse into a run, holding on for dear life. He couldn't hear the screaming now and he was thankful for that. He knew the longer the wolf stayed with Trevor the better chance he would have of outrunning it on his horse. Looking over his shoulder he couldn't see the yellow eyes following. As his horse crested the ridge above the camp, Tommy looked back and saw the demon coming for him only a hundred yards away. Screaming, he rode down off the ridge at a dead run. Feeling weak and very faint he hung onto the saddle horn with both hands, almost lying on the horse's neck. Then everything went black.

Hearing the rifle shot, miners from the camp began to gather by the corrals. "Who could still be out there?" they asked as people started to gather.

"It must be Trevor and Tommy," a logger replied. "They were supposed to come down behind the wagon but they never showed up. Trevor would cut trees all night if you let him. I'm going out there to help if I can!" the logger yelled, rifle in his hand.

"Hold on and we will all go with you," several miners replied. Breaking off from the others a group of about a dozen strong, all armed with rifles, started up the ridge. When they were halfway up the ridge they looked up and saw a terrified horse burst over the top with a rider hanging on like a rag doll. Scrambling to get out of the way, the men watched as the horse and rider raced past and down into camp. Miners at the camp caught the horse before it could run headlong down the street.

"This man is bleeding badly!" a man said as he pulled Tommy from the horse. Carefully several miners took Tommy to a large tent where a makeshift doctor tended people.

"Put him over there," the doctor said as they brought him in. The doctor had a large table made from a slab of wood covered with a tablecloth. Two lamps hung over the table providing plenty of light. As the miners lay Tommy gently on the table the doctor rolled him on his side, exposing his back.

"Oh my God!" several people, including the doctor, muttered as they saw how his shirt and back were ripped to shreds. As the doctor cut away the bloody strips of Tommy's shirt he could see claw marks as well as a deep bite marks on his back. Carefully washing the wound, he was glad Tommy was unconscious as he began sewing him up.

It didn't take long for the news to spread around the camp of another attack and possible killing. Hearing about the wounded man,

Scotty went to the hospital tent to try and talk to him. When he got there the doctor had just finished bandaging his wounds.

"Can I talk to him?" Scotty asked the doctor.

"As soon as you help me put him in that cot," the doctor answered. Scotty lifted the boy easily and placed him gently on his side on the cot. He saw the boy's eyelids flutter and try to open.

"What's his name?" Scotty asked.

"I heard it was Tommy," the doctor replied.

"Tommy, Tommy, can you hear me?" Scotty asked in a gentle voice. He saw Tommy's eyes open and saw they were terrified. "Don't worry Tommy, you're safe here. You're in the hospital tent at the camp now. There is nothing to be frightened of here," Scotty said gently. Tommy looked wide-eyed all around before looking at Scotty and relaxing a little.

"Where am I?" Tommy asked in a shaken voice.

"You are in the hospital tent back at camp," Scotty replied. "Do you remember what happened to you?" Scotty asked in a concerned voice.

Tommy looked terrified again, his eyes as big as saucers. "Wolf!" he screamed. "Wolf!" Frightened, he tried to sit up but Scotty gently held him until he calmed down.

"That is probably as much as you should question him tonight," the doctor told Scotty. "Maybe in the morning he will feel stronger and can tell you more." Nodding his head in agreement, Scotty watched Tommy close his eyes and fall unconscious. Leaving the hospital tent, Scotty wondered how a wolf could do all the terrible things he had seen lately. *Maybe what he needed was a good stiff shot of whiskey and a beer chaser to help sort these things out in his mind,* he thought as he walked up the street towards the saloon. As he approached the saloon he noticed the piano was not playing. It was too early yet for it to be silent, he thought as he walked through the tent flap. As his eyes got adjusted to the bright lamplight, he noticed a crowd gathered around the bar. A small man in a fur hat, wearing buckskins and moccasins was doing all the talking.

"I'm telling you, all the stories are true!" he told the crowd as he removed his short-stemmed pipe from his teeth. "I heard old Running Bear tell about the legend of the wolf people when I was a pup. That was a long time ago," he said, laughing, and showing them his long gray beard. "Running Bear was a great warrior but I saw him quiver in fear as he talked about them."

"Talked about who?" a voice in the crowd yelled.

"About the wolf people, that's who!" he replied matter-of-factly. "They were fierce warriors during the day but during the full moon they turned into wolf demons, unstoppable as they killed and ate their victims." Everybody was quiet, listening intently to what he was saying. "It is said they took their enemies to a sacred cave on this mountain and feasted on their flesh."

"No ..." someone in the crowd muttered.

"What did they look like?" a voice asked.

"I've never seen one, mind you," the man said, removing his fur hat, "but my guess is they look as normal as you and me, until the full moon glows in the night sky. Then they must be terrible to behold," the old-timer said, putting his hat back on and puffing on his pipe.

"What happened to the wolf people?" a voice from the crowd asked.

"Nobody really knows, the first time anyone ever set foot in this country was when this silver mine was discovered. Another thing," the old-timer said, squinting his beady eyes and looking very serious. "You can't kill the wolves with lead bullets; only a silver bullet in their demon heart will kill them forever."

"Silver," the murmur went up in the crowd. "Are you sure?"

"As sure as I can be," the old timer replied, puffing on his pipe.

"Was anyone here before silver was discovered?" a voice asked.

"Just the two owners, a half-breed and his Indian mother," another voice answered.

"Now just a minute!" Scotty said in a deep booming voice. "This is starting to go too far. I happen to know the two owners personally and know them to be fine people. I'll take it personal if anyone uses their names when discussing this silly wolf legend again! Understand?" he said in a booming voice. The saloon was so quiet you could hear a mouse walking across the floor. "Good!" he exclaimed. "Now let me buy you all a beer and let's not worry about people who turn into wolves anymore. We have got our hands full worrying about a bear or a wolf that keeps attacking people." Pushing through the crowd he walked up to the old timer and introduced himself. "My name is Scotty," he said in a deep voice.

"Tyler is the name," the man said, shaking Scotty hand.

"Do you believe in the wolf legend?" Scotty asked him quietly.

"You mean about the part where people turn into wolves and eat other people? I'm not sure," Tyler said, removing the stem of his pipe from his mouth. "It seems kind of far-fetched but I've talked to people who lived around these mountains all their lives who won't step one foot on this mountain. Not for all the silver in the world." Scotty drank two beers while talking to Tyler. "I like you, Scotty," Tyler said as he finished his beer. "I'm sorry if I offended you earlier."

"No not at all, I just got offended when the owners were dragged into the legend. I've never met finer people."

"Well, if you think they are okay then they must be," Tyler said. "Have they lived here long?"

"All their lives," Scotty replied.

"I know they are super-nice people Scotty and because I like you, I'll give you one word of advice. Keep your eye on them!" Slapping Scotty on his big shoulder, Tyler turned and was gone before Scotty could reply.

"Keep an eye on them?" Scotty muttered under his breath. Thinking of Tashina's beauty, he muttered to himself, "I would like to be part of the family." Scotty went back to his bunk and tried to get some sleep. He was tired as he lay his big body down on the bunk and closed his eyes. Thinking of what Tyler had said about keeping his eye on them, he slowly fell asleep. The rest of the night he tossed and turned, mumbling to himself. He saw Tashina smiling at him, her fawn eyes pleading with him to come closer. She reached her small hand out to him, telling him not to be afraid.

"I won't hurt you Scotty, you know that," she said in a seductive voice. "Come to me Scotty, take my hand and I'll take you away with me," she said, still holding her hand out to him. Scotty wanted to hold her but was frightened of her at the same time. Reaching out, he took her dainty hand in his and gazing into her beautiful fawn eyes, pulled her to him. Suddenly her fawn eyes turned fiery yellow and growling she turned into a hideous wolf creature. In an instant she bit his arm

81

savagely and he jerked back in pain and fear. Flinging himself off the bunk, he hit the ground hard and woke up.

"What a dream," he muttered. "It seemed so real!" He was shaking a little and then realized he was soaked in sweat. *I must have been dreaming for a while*, he thought to himself. Feeling cold, he lay down and covered up in his blankets. Every time he closed his eyes he saw Tashina turn into the wolf and bite his arm. He lay awake the rest of the night, getting up just as the pre-dawn light was filling the sky. Deciding to go to the mine early in the morning, he hoped being busy would keep his mind off Tashina and the wolf. Getting dressed, he left the tent and started walking towards the mine. Maybe a brisk walk in the cool morning air would make him feel better. Suddenly he remembered Tommy. He really needed to talk to the boy about what had happened last night.

Walking back into camp, he went to the hospital tent. Opening the flap, he went inside and quietly over to Tommy's cot.

"Tommy wake up," he said, gently shaking Tommy's shoulder. Tommy's eyes opened and he looked at Scotty.

"What do you want?" he asked.

"I want to talk to you about what happened last night."

"Trevor is dead!" Tommy said in a sad whisper.

"We won't know for sure until the search party gets back."

"He is dead!" Tommy said again. "I saw the wolf kill him as I rode away."

"Was there one wolf or a pack of wolves?" Scotty asked.

Tommy looked up at him and said, "It was a huge wolf with fiery yellow eyes that stood on its hind legs!"

"Are you sure?" Scotty asked in a non-believing voice.

"I saw it stand and look at us before Trevor shot it!"

"He shot the wolf?"

"Yes, several times, but it still kept coming, hardly flinching as the bullets struck it!" While Scotty was talking to Tommy, the doctor came over to change his bandages that were stained in blood. Removing the bandage, he looked shocked and muttered under his breath.

"What's that doctor?" Scotty asked.

"His wounds are healing very fast, I've never seen anything like it!"

"What do you mean?"

"See for yourself," the doctor replied, holding the bandage open. Scotty looked at Tommy's back and thought the wounds looked at least a week old.

"That's hard to believe!" he muttered. Looking at Tommy he said, "At the rate you are healing, it won't be long before you are up and running around again."

Tommy smiled and replied, "I wish the pain of seeing my friend killed would heal as fast."

Scotty placed his hand on Tommy's shoulder saying, "Get well fast, Tommy, and if you need anything, tell the doctor and he will let me know."

"I'll let you know as soon as I know," the doctor replied. Leaving the tent, Scotty headed again towards the mine.

Confronting the Wolves

Above the horizon, the sky had a soft red glow, promising the sun was soon to appear. The morning air was chilly as Scotty pulled up the collar of his coat. Hands in his pockets, he walked quickly, enjoying the early morning exercise. Once on top of the ridge, he stopped for a moment and watched the first golden rays of sunshine burst over the horizon and onto the mountainside. Looking down at the cabin below, he thought again of Tashina and his dream. Then he saw her bathing in the creek. Unable to resist the temptation to see her again, he walked down off the ridge towards the cabin.

Tashina sensed someone was on the ridge watching her bathe. She knew from the scent it was Scotty. She watched him walk down off the ridge towards her as she hurriedly washed the blood from her body and put her dress on. Scotty waved at her and she waved back as she walked towards the cabin.

"Morning," he said as he met her next to the cabin.

"Morning to you," she replied. "You're out really early this morning. What's going on?" she asked in a concerned voice.

"Let's go in before you get cold and I will tell you," he replied. "You shouldn't be out here in the cold morning air, especially bathing in the creek."

"Oh, you saw me!" she said, shaking her finger at him while she smiled.

"How could I not see a beautiful flower bathing in the first rays of the morning sun?" he told her from his heart.

Opening the door of the cabin, she invited him in. The cabin was warm and cozy as Scotty took his coat off and laid it next to the door. Grabbing the coffee pot, Tashina started to go outside but Scotty stopped her.

"Don't you think you have already been cold enough? I'll go get fresh water for the coffee," he said, opening the cabin door and going to the stream. Quickly he filled the pot with fresh water and then headed back to the cabin.

"What's Scotty doing here?" Chato asked Tashina as he yawned.

"I'm not sure," Tashina answered. "I had just gotten back and was bathing when he walked down off the ridge."

"Lucky you were here already, I would hate to try to explain where you were this time of the morning." The door opened and Scotty came in carrying the pot filled with water. Handing it to Tashina, he rubbed his hands over the fire in the fireplace.

"It's chilly out there," he told them, trying to warm up.

"You should have worn your coat," Tashina said.

""You're a fine one to talk, washing in the freezing water," Scotty replied with a smile.

"Is something wrong?" Chato asked as he walked up to the table and sat across from Scotty.

"We had another attack last night and probably another killing," Scotty told them in a concerned voice.

"What happened?" Chato asked.

"This time we have an eye witness who saw a huge wolf attack him and his partner."

"Do you mean he is still alive?" Chato said in wonder.

"Yes, I talked to him this morning after he had rested some and he swears it was a demon wolf with yellow eyes that walked on its hind legs."

"You're kidding me!" Chato said in disbelief.

"No, that's exactly what the kid said," replied Scotty. "He was attacked and then saw the wolf kill his partner before he escaped on a fast horse."

"Do you believe this kid?" Tashina asked in a quiet voice.

"I'm not sure what to believe," Scotty replied. Tashina put fresh coffee grounds in the pot and then placed it on the fire.

"There is something else, isn't there Scotty?" she asked, looking deep into his eyes. "What is it?"

"It's the legend about this place," he replied. "With a wolf on the loose, old-timers are talking about wolf people who turn into wolves during the full moon," he said in a concerned voice. "I wanted to warn the two of you early this morning in case anyone gives you any trouble."

"What do you mean?" Tashina asked.

"Everyone knows the two of you have lived on this mountain all your lives. In blind fear they might accuse you both of being wolf people."

"Do you believe we are wolves during the full moon?" Tashina asked him openly, looking deep into his eyes. She could see Scotty was hurt by the question and wished she hadn't asked it.

"You know better than that!" Scotty replied in a hurt voice. "Would I be here now if I thought something as foolish as that?"

"I'm sorry, Scotty," Tashina said, walking in front of him and placing her hands on his shoulders. "I should have known without asking you wouldn't believe such lies about us." Sitting down at the table, Tashina listened closely.

"Something else happened," Scotty said. "The boy Tommy who was attacked by the wolf had terrible cuts and bite marks on his back when they found him last night. This morning when I visited him they looked as if they were at least a week old or more. The doctor said he has never seen anything like it before."

"That's strange," Chato muttered, looking at Tashina. Once the coffee was brewed, Tashina poured everyone a cup. Drinking her coffee, she could barely remember the boy who had gotten away. She was surprised the wolf was distracted enough to let that happen. It had never happened before. Sipping her coffee, she wondered what it meant that the wounds were healing so quickly. It reminded her of her own wounds she had received last night that was almost completely healed now.

"Mother, are you listening?" Chato asked, finally getting his mother's attention.

"What?" Tashina said, looking at Chato and Scotty.

"Scotty says to stay low until Sam gets here and he can straighten things out."

"Sounds fine to me, I wasn't planning on going anywhere," Tashina answered, playing with her coffee cup. Finishing his coffee, Scotty got up and put his coat on.

"I better get to the mine and get things lined out." Saying goodbye, he left the cabin, closing the door behind him.

"A witness!" Chato said in an irritated voice. "How did you let the boy escape you?"

"I'm not sure, I think the wolf took too long with the first kill and never had enough time to catch the boy before he entered the camp."

"From what Scotty says we are being blamed now because of the legend. I knew it would happen sooner or later if we weren't careful!" Chato said in an angry voice.

"You can control the wolf in you at will but I can't!" his mother told him. "I have been lucky to control the wolf in me as well as I have!" Tashina was tired and going to her bed, laid down and fell into a deep sleep. Chato watched her sleeping peacefully for a while and then went outside in the bright sunshine to chop some much-needed firewood. He wouldn't go to the mine today, he told himself.

If Scotty was right there might be trouble, he thought as he searched the surrounding countryside for riders. Seeing none, he went behind the cabin and started chopping firewood.

Tashina was exhausted, and after falling into a deep sleep, she dreamed she was the wolf and was chasing the boy. Quickly she was gaining on the frightened horse and its rider when suddenly she sprang alongside the horse and reached up to tear the rider from the saddle. Suddenly, there was Scotty standing before her, smiling. She was herself, dressed in a beautiful dress as she reached out her hand towards him. She was talking to him softly and watched as he hesitated and then placed his hand around hers, pulling her to him. Holding his hand she came closer and then suddenly turned into the wolf and savagely sank her teeth into his arm. Startled, she awoke and sat up quickly on the bed. It took her a moment before she realized it was only a dream. Holding her head in her hands she tried to shake off the nightmare. She could hear the chopping of an ax behind the cabin and knew it was Chato cutting firewood. Lying back down, she closed her eyes and listening to the chopping of the ax, fell back to sleep.

As Chato cut the wood to length and split them, he thought about the mine and how any day now the miners would break into the cave.

Soon his people would be free and they would drive everyone from the mountain. He thought about how nice it would be to be rich from the silver and live in a mansion somewhere, letting someone else cut your firewood for you. He knew his mother would never leave the mountain. He could live in the cities, he told himself. He had control of the wolf inside him and only let it out when he wanted. Swinging the ax, he watched it bite deep into the log, chopping a chip off. Pulling it free, he swung it again cutting even deeper into the other side of the notch. What about the boy? He thought to himself as he swung the ax. His wounds were healing faster than normal. "What does it mean?" he muttered under his breath as he swung the ax. No one had ever escaped them before or their ancestors that he knew of. The boy was healing almost as fast as the wolf could. This puzzled him. Maybe he should visit the boy when things cooled down a little. Stopping to catch his breath he heard riders coming down the ridge. Carrying his ax, he walked to the front of the cabin just as the six riders rode up. He looked at each man but never recognized anyone.

"What can I do for you?" he asked in a deep voice.

"Have you been home all morning?" a heavyset man with fat cheeks asked.

"Reckon so," Chato replied.

"Tell him about Trevor and Tommy!" a gruff looking man wearing a wide-brimmed hat said.

"Alright, alright!" the heavyset man replied. "Last night a wolf creature attacked two loggers, wounding one man and killing and eating the other. The wounded logger, Tommy, rode into town last night tore up pretty bad. This morning a search party went to find Trevor and found mostly bones and bloody clothes."

"Do you think it was the bear again?" Chato asked.

"We think it was you, or your Indian mother!" a man in buckskins said, spitting a stream of tobacco towards Chato.

"You think what?" Chato said, starting to get angry.

"You heard me!" the man snarled. "I said we think you and your mother have been doing all the killings! As soon as the full moon lights the night sky you turn into wolves and hunt, killing everything you find." Chato was very angry and started raising his ax when the door of the cabin opened and Tashina stepped out holding a loaded rifle.

"Morning everyone!" she said in a polite voice. "What can I do for you today?"

"We came to see what you two did last night," the heavyset man replied.

"Well, let's see," Tashina said, taking one hand from the rifle and placing a finger on her cheek as she tried to remember. "I remember, we turned into wolves and ran howling over the mountainside, killing whatever we found!"

"Now see here," the heavyset man stammered, "That's not funny! A man was killed last night and a boy lays wounded in our camp below."

"You damn right that's not funny!" Tashina said with a snarl. "No matter what we say you aren't going to believe us, so we may as well say what you want to hear!" Lifting her rifle, she leveled it at the group saying "Anybody else want to accuse us of being wolves like the legend says?" Seeing the rifle pointed their way and the crazed look in Tashina's eyes, they all quietly shook their heads. "You people make me sick!" Tashina snarled, still pointing her rifle at them. "Instead of combing the countryside to find whatever killed your friend, you find it easier to accuse an Indian woman and her son of the murder! Look at this hand!" she said, holding up her small brown hand. "Does this look like it could turn into a wolf large enough to hurt full grown men like you?" All the men were getting nervous and feeling foolish when the heavyset man spoke.

"Ma'am, I apologize for what has been said here this morning!"

"Say goodbye!" Tashina said in an angry voice. "Maybe next time you come to visit we can have coffee and a bite to eat. For now, I think you gentlemen have outstayed your welcome." Seeing she was serious, the riders turned and rode away back towards their camp. As they neared the top of the ridge they met a rider coming towards the cabin. The riders stopped and talked briefly to the rider before going on their way. The lone rider left them and rode down to the cabin.

"Now what?" Chato muttered to his mother. As the rider rode up they saw it was Sam Jenkins. He looked flustered and out of place on the back of a horse.

"Morning, partners!" he yelled as he climbed down from his pony. "That looked like a nasty crowd I met at the top of the ridge a second ago. They said your mother really put them in their place," he said to Chato.

"Put your horse in the corral and come on in," Tashina told him as she opened the cabin door and went inside.

"How was your trip?" Chato asked, following Sam to the corral.

"It wasn't any shorter than it was the last time I was here," Sam said laughing. "It sounds like you have had trouble with a killer bear or wolf, and now people are starting to believe in the old legend," Sam said, unsaddling and putting his pony in the corral. Removing a leather case full of papers from his saddle he walked back to the cabin following Chato. "I still can't get over how beautiful it is here!"

Once inside the cabin, he sat down at the table while Tashina brought him some coffee.

"It's good to see my partners again," he told them with a smile. "Wait until you see how much money we have made from our mine!" he exclaimed. Once everyone was sitting at the table, he opened the case and removed a stack of papers. "These are all the bills we have acquired thus far to keep the mine running. This is a bank deposit slip for the amount of forty thousand dollars in your names." Chato took the deposit slip and saw it was for the amount Sam had said.

"We thought maybe you would pay us our share in gold coins," Chato replied.

"Heavens no!" Sam exclaimed. "Not only would it be hard to pack up the mountain, it wouldn't be safe once you got it here."

"What do you mean?" Tashina asked.

"I mean once the ruffians down below knew of a gold stash on this mountain they wouldn't stop until you were dead and your gold was gone. You saw how they got worked up over a silly legend," he told them.

"We would like to review the bills with you," Chato told him.

Sam looked surprised, but smiled and said, "Fine," as he sorted them out on the table.

"I'm going to get some fresh air," Tashina told them. "You two review the bills together, you don't need me."

Getting to her feet, Tashina placed her hand on Chato's shoulder and then went outside the cabin, closing the door behind her. Once outside she breathed deep of the fresh mountain air. It was still early afternoon and fall colors were everywhere. Aspen trees bordered the tall pines all across the mountain with their leaves of yellow and orange. The chalky white bark of the aspens were covered with black marks extending to their branches. The pines were all shades of green in the afternoon sun and changed as the shadows fell across them. Tashina felt trapped on her beautiful mountain. The people who had come here were choking the life out of it. All the game had been driven off with the pressure of the camp hunters. Looking at the peaks above the mine, she hoped it would soon be over.

Chato, unable to read, reviewed the bills with Sam, insisting that he read them to him and explain them. Before Sam left, Chato had him promise to deposit ten thousand more dollars in their account. Chato caught Sam reading an error that Sam never noticed. Sam was fuming! How could a man unable to read find one of the charges he had invented to give himself more money! Next time he would be more careful. Chato was not a stupid man.

As the days sped quickly by without any more killings, things began to settle down. Chato went to the mine every day now, sure the miners were going to break into the cave. Sam had been a bother to Scotty until he had almost worn out his welcome and then went back down the mountain with the next pack train. "Our business needs me back in town," he told Chato and Tashina as he waved goodbye.

Last of their Kind

The next day when Chato went to the mine, he met Scotty, who was looking very puzzled.

"What is it?" he asked.

"I'm not sure," Scotty replied. "We broke into a huge cave in the mountain this morning. When the powder smoke from the blasting cleared, we discovered a huge cavern." Chato was almost beside himself with joy.

"Where are you going?" Scotty asked, as Chato fled down the mountain.

"To get mother!" Chato yelled back. When Chato ran into the cabin and Tashina saw the look on his face she knew they had blasted into the cave. Without saying a word she grabbed her jacket and followed Chato back to the mine.

"I can't believe it!" Chato muttered to her as they scrambled up the ridge. Scotty met them at the mine entrance.

"Come to see the cavern, huh?" he said to Tashina with a smile. Carrying an oil lamp, he led them down the long tunnel. It got darker and damper the farther they went. Finally, Tashina could see several lamps moving around in front of them. All the way in, they had been following two steel rails, fastened to large pieces of lumber. Now Tashina could see why. Miners were busy shoveling dirt and ore into an ore cart made mostly from wood with iron wheels that followed the iron tracks.

"Be careful here, Tashina," Scotty said, "for all we know the whole thing could cave in at any second. We almost missed it completely," he said, pointing to the three-foot diameter hole leading into the cavern.

"Are you sure you want to go in there?" Scotty asked Tashina, seeing that she was very excited. Tashina nodded her head and was the first one through the hole and into the cavern. Chato took a lamp from one of the miners and followed her in. Holding the lamp high, they waited for Scotty.

"My God!" Tashina exclaimed. She turned to Chato and whispered, "It's just like I remember." *They were at the far end of the cavern*, Tashina thought as she walked towards the upper end. *Where were her people?* her mind screamed. The cavern was over one hundred yards long, thirty to forty yards wide, and at least thirty yards high in spots.

"No ... no ..." Tashina muttered as she saw shrunken, mummified bodies lying on the cavern floor.

"My God, look at this!" Scotty exclaimed as he saw the shrunken bodies. "People must have been trapped in here alive!" The farther they went the more bodies they found. Some were nothing but bones.

"They were eaten by the others!" Chato exclaimed, pointing to teeth marks on the stark white bones. Reaching the front of the cavern, they saw the huge boulders and rocks closing off the entrance.

"There must have been a huge blast to cause a cave in like this," Scotty said, looking in wonder at the boulders blocking the entrance. Tears were welling up in Tashina's eyes and she turned to go back before Scotty saw her. It was then she noticed the claw marks deep in the walls of the cavern as high as her people could reach. The marks were scratched in solid stone and in some places were over an inch deep. *How terrible it must have been for them*, she thought, *trapped for years in total darkness, eating their own kind to stay alive.* She remembered the mournful howling she used to hear coming from the mountain and began to cry.

"What's wrong?" Scotty asked in a concerned voice as he went to her side.

"Nothing!" she cried as she ran out of the cavern and into the mineshaft.

Scotty looked at Chato who shrugged his shoulders and said, "Seeing all the suffering that happened in this cavern was just too much for her."

"I guess you're right," Scotty replied as he held his lamp higher to see better. "Terrible things have happened in this cavern, that's for sure. I'm going to head out and see if I can't comfort her," he told

93

Chato. "Don't stay too long, it won't be long until they blast again." Chato turned, and holding his light high, looked at his people lying dead before him. For twenty-five years they had been trapped in this place and now that he had finally come to set them free, they were gone. His plans were ruined without them at his side.

"Too late …" he muttered in pain. "We are too late …"

Holding the light high, he felt tears starting to well up in his eyes as they changed to fiery yellow. He felt the wolf take over his body, and almost let his body change before coming to his senses and stopping it. Saddened beyond belief, he left the cavern. He gave his lamp back to a miner, and made his way towards the small light at the end of the tunnel. Once in the sunlight again he squinted his eyes to see, waiting for them to adjust to the bright light. Then he saw Scotty walking back to the entrance.

"She doesn't want to talk or be bothered," Scotty told him in a sad voice. "I shouldn't have let her go into the cavern!"

"Don't worry, Scotty, she is tough, and will be her old self in no time," Chato said, still grieving himself. "I'll go down and check on her."

"Tell her if she needs anything to let me know!"

"She is not sure what she needs right now," Chato told him, walking towards the cabin with his hands in his pockets. "And neither am I," he groaned to himself.

Once back at the cabin he found Tashina sobbing on her bed. She looked up and saw him when he opened the door and then started sobbing again.

"We are the last of our people!" she said. "How will we ever take our mountain back now?" she asked wiping her eyes.

"Mother, we will figure something out, we always do," Chato replied.

"When the moon comes again, I will turn the wolf loose on the camps below!" she said with a snarl. "Then they will flee for their lives!"

"If you do that it will be the end of us and you know it," Chato answered, starting to become upset. "We will work this out together! We may not have our people behind us, but we do have their blood in our bodies. You and I are the wolf people now, just like we have always been. Together we can feast on the flesh of their bodies for as long as they remain on this mountain."

Late that afternoon just before dark, Scotty knocked on the cabin door. Opening the door Tashina invited Scotty in. Holding his hat in his big hands, he invited them to join him for supper.

"I know you feel bad about the sadness in the cavern," he said to Tashina in a tender voice. "Will you and Chato please come to supper with me? I know we can make the day end better than it started." Pleading with his eyes, he was startled when she told him yes. "You will?" he asked in disbelief.

"When should we meet you?" Tashina asked.

"Soon," he said, getting all excited. "Just let me have a few minutes to clean up after I get back and I'll be ready." He was so excited he was crushing the brim of his derby hat in his big hands.

"This time I'm buying," Chato stated. "We need to start spending a little of our hard-earned money," he said, smiling at his mother.

"I had better get going," Scotty said putting his hat back on while opening the cabin door. "You know where to meet me, right?"

"Yes, I remember," Chato replied.

The last rays of the evening sun were covering the mountainside when Chato and Tashina descended the ridge to the miner's camps.

"We must be careful," Chato told her as she walked at his side. "We may still be suspects of the killings."

"If they only knew," Tashina said, smiling. Entering the camp just as darkness fell, Chato led them to Scotty's tent.

"Wait here, mother, and I will see if he is ready." Opening the tent flap he saw Scotty looking all spruced up, coming towards him.

"Are you hungry?" Scotty asked in a booming voice as he stepped outside the tent.

"I am," Chato answered. "What about you, mother?"

Tashina looked around the camp quickly and then at Scotty and said, "I feel as if I could eat the whole camp," in a playful voice.

"Well how about we start with a big steak first?" Scotty said, holding his arm out to Tashina. Taking his arm, she smiled and laughed, telling him that would be a good place to start. Oil lamps and a few campfires lit up the whole camp, making it glow in the darkness. Scotty led them to the dining tent and beamed with pride as he walked inside, Tashina on his arm. The tent was filled with cigar and pipe smoke and the delicious smell of steaks cooking over a grill. Everyone was talking and laughing, enjoying their dinners. As Scotty and the two mine owners entered the tent, the talking stopped. Chato saw how they looked at Tashina and himself and thought there might be trouble. Going to an empty table near the back of the tent, Scotty pulled a chair out for Tashina and then sat down next to her. Chato could still feel their eyes watching him as he sat down at the table. He could hear the whispers with his wolf hearing and knew his mother did also.

"Wolf people, they turn into wolves during the full moon. They are the mine owners," he heard the whispers say. "They lived here all their lives. Sure she is small and pretty, but is a savage when the moon is full."

"I don't believe a damn word of it," he heard a miner say. "Scotty would know if they were demons, wouldn't he?"

"If they turn into wolves, why aren't they wolves now?" a voice whispered.

"Because the moon is not full," another voice whispered.

"It's just a scare tactic to keep everyone away from the silver," said another voice quietly.

Danny appeared in his apron with several pitchers of beer for the miners. As he poured their mugs full, he could hear some of the whispers. "You are like children," he told them quietly so Scotty's table couldn't hear. "I know for a damn fact that Chato there ate steaks with Scotty in this very tent the other night when the moon was full! The night the man was killed by the corrals," he whispered. "He was with Scotty most of the night at that table and the only thing he wolfed down was his steak and baked potatoes." Glaring at the whisperers, he wiped his hands on his apron and went to Scotty's table.

"Good evening, ma'am," he said to Tashina and nodded to Chato and Scotty. Everyone went back to eating their dinners and enjoying each other's company and once again the tent was noisy. Chato looked at his mother and could tell she had heard everything.

"We are hungry, Danny," Scotty said. "Bring us three large steaks and the works."

"How do you like your steaks?" Looking at Scotty he said, "Well done." Scotty nodded his head. Turning to Chato, Danny thought for a moment and then said, "Bloody rare, right?"

Chato smiled and said, "You must have a good memory!"

"Sometimes I just get lucky."

Tashina looked up from the table at Danny and said, "Make mine bloody rare also."

"Bring us a pitcher of beer while we wait," Scotty told Danny as he went to the back of the tent. Remembering Tashina, he politely asked, "Is beer okay or would you like something else?"

Tashina smiled and said beer would be fine. It wasn't long until Chato and Tashina's steaks were ready and Danny brought them to the table.

"Yours will be done in a few minutes," he told Scotty as he left.

"I can't eat all of this!" Tashina exclaimed.

"Sure you can," Scotty answered in a gentle voice. "It will help you get your strength back after being sick for so long."

Chato, already eating his steak with blood dripping down his lips, looked at his mother and told her, "There is nothing like fresh meat warmed over a grill." He saw her smile wickedly as he licked the blood from his lips. Tashina's steak was brown on the outside but the minute she cut it with her knife it began to bleed.

"Mmmm …" she said as she chewed a piece of the bloody meat.

"You like it?" Scotty asked. Nodding her head, she wiped the blood from her lips. "That's great, I was hoping I could cheer you up some." Scotty finished drinking his beer and watched Chato and Tashina wolf down their steaks. Just when he thought he was going to starve, Danny brought his steak and three huge baked potatoes.

"How do you like them so far?" Danny asked.

"Well I just got mine so how would I know?" Scotty asked, laughing.

"Not you, you big moose, I'm asking these two!"

"My name is Tashina and this is Chato," Tashina answered. "My steak is excellent!"

"Great!" Danny exclaimed. "Let me know if you need anything else," he told them as he left the table. Tashina hadn't realized she was so hungry until she started eating her steak. Chato was right, the steak was very delicious. As she ate her steak, she watched Scotty. *He was such a nice man, much like Jack,* she thought as she chewed a piece of the juicy steak. She looked at the others she had heard whispering earlier and knew she could easily feed on their flesh when she turned wolf but what about Scotty?

Lately she wasn't sure! She knew the wolf in her would kill him easily, if it got the chance. But the question was, is that what she wanted? She watched him, happy as a young boy with a new toy as he ate his steak. Stabbing a bloody piece of steak with her fork, she popped it in her mouth and was thinking about Scotty when she sensed the presence of a wolf and it wasn't Chato. Almost choking with shock, she looked up and saw a young man enter the tent and stand in the lamplight. Chato sensed it at the same time and dropped his fork when he saw the boy.

"Scotty!" the young man yelled as he saw Scotty.

"Tommy," Scotty answered waving him over. "What are you doing out of the hospital tent?"

"I'm all healed up now, and was hoping you would give me a job."

"A job, what do you mean?"

"Well, I don't want to go back to the forest after what happened last time, so I figured maybe I could work for you in the mine." Tommy looked at Chato and Tashina, feeling uncomfortable. It felt like he knew these people or had met them sometime in the past.

Scotty saw Tommy with a puzzled look and said. "Excuse me folks. Tommy, this is Tashina and Chato, the owners of the silver mine. Tommy was attacked and escaped the hideous creature that killed his partner," he told Tashina. Chato stood up and shook Tommy's hand, inviting him to sit down. As Tommy sat down, Tashina looked deep into his eyes and saw the wolf.

"Are you hungry?" Chato asked. "I'm buying."

"Sure, I'm always hungry, and even more so lately." Chato waved to Danny and asked Tommy how he wanted his steak cooked? Looking at what was left of Chato's bloody steak, Tommy licked his lips and said, "Just like yours would be fine." When Danny, arrived Chato told him they needed two more bloody rare steaks and a beer mug for Tommy. Both Tashina and Chato were startled to feel the presence of another wolf. They watched Tommy closely and when Danny brought the steaks, saw how eagerly he ate the bloody pieces. Chato had finished his steak and started on the second one, asking Tashina if she wanted some.

"No thank you," she replied. "I've still got a big piece of mine to eat yet."

"How about that job?" Tommy asked as he wolfed down his steak.

"Are you sure you're able to work?" Scotty asked. "Your back was pretty torn up."

"Nothing but a few scars now," Tommy replied. As Tommy sliced off another piece of steak and stuck it with his fork, he saw blood show on the sides. "You know what's weird?" he said. "This is the first time I have ever had steak this rare, usually I always have well done." Seeing Scotty's well-done steak Tommy smiled, saying, "You don't know what you're missing, Scotty."

"No thank you," Scotty replied, smiling at Tashina. "There has to be at least one of us that knows what a fire is for." Once they were done with their steaks, Danny passed out cigars to everyone. Tashina declined a cigar and sat back relaxing, watching Tommy. *Maybe her mistake wasn't such a big mistake after all*, she thought to herself.

"Meet me at my tent at dawn tomorrow," Scotty told Tommy. "I'll give you a try in the mine. Have you got a place to stay?"

"Yeah, as long as I can pay," Tommy replied. Putting his half-smoked cigar into his mouth, Scotty reached into his pocket, squinting at the cigar smoke burning his eyes, and pulled out a gold coin.

Tossing it to Tommy he said, "Here is an advance, make sure to use it to pay for a bunk and a warm place to stay."

Catching the coin, Tommy looked very sincere and said, "Thanks, Scotty, I really appreciate it."

"You had better get some sleep if you're going to work hard for me all day tomorrow," Scotty said. Standing up, Tommy thanked everyone for the supper and left. Tashina was touched by Scotty's kindness, saying nothing she reached out and laid her hand on his. Startled, he turned and blushed as she smiled at him. Thanking him with her eyes, she pulled her hand away and asked Chato if he was ready to go. He looked up from his partially-smoked cigar and told her to go ahead. He would follow as soon as he was done.

"Let me walk you home?" Scotty asked Tashina.

"Go ahead, mother, I won't be too long," Chato told her.

Smiling at Scotty she said with a laugh, "It's a long walk, are you sure you're up to it?"

"Try and stop me!" Scotty replied with a grin.

Standing, Scotty reached into his pocket to pay for the meal when Chato said quickly, "This time dinner is on us."

"Sounds good to me," Scotty replied. Tashina stood as Scotty pulled her chair back and taking his arm followed him out of the dining tent. Chato sat back in his chair, relaxing as he finished smoking his cigar. His mind was spinning, thinking about the wolf he sensed in Tommy and what that might mean. Could it be that when bitten or scratched by the wolf, a human would turn into the wolf? Never before had anyone escaped the wolf. This was the break they needed after discovering that their people were dead. He would watch the boy and see what happened on the next full moon. If he turned wolf and attacked the mining camp, it would look as if he was the wolf all the time. Smiling a wicked smile, Chato thought to himself, *this is getting better all the time.*

All the way up the ridge from camp, Scotty tried desperately to think of something to talk about but couldn't think of anything. Tashina could sense his frustration and as they neared the top of the ridge, she looked up into the star-filled sky, exclaiming, "What a beautiful evening this is!"

"It is pretty, isn't it?" Scotty said, stopping at the ridge top to enjoy it.

"How many stars do you think there are?" Tashina asked, looking up at the night sky.

"Thousands! Maybe millions! There is one thing that would make the night sky even more beautiful tonight," Scotty told her.

"What's that?"

"A full moon," Scotty replied. Tashina's eyes twinkled as she looked at Scotty.

"Do you really think so?"

"Sure, the moon always brightens up the sky and lets us see things more clearly." Laughing at what Scotty said, Tashina let him put his arms around her.

"Maybe you're right Scotty, maybe you're right."

He could feel her trembling and asked, "Are you cold?"

"No, I'm not cold, I'm not sure why I'm trembling."

"Well, we had better get you inside before you get sick again." Tashina enjoyed the walk from the ridge top to the cabin with Scotty's arm around her. Once inside the cabin, Tashina started to build a fire while Scotty went out and brought in an armload of wood. Dropping the wood on the floor next to the door, he told Tashina he had best be going and he really enjoyed her company.

"Thank you," Tashina told him, "for making what started as a very bad day into a wonderful evening."

"Maybe we can do it again?" Scotty said to her in a hopeful voice.

"I would really like that," Tashina replied. As Scotty left and closed the door behind him, Tashina added wood to the fire and listened to his footsteps walking away. How would she deal with Scotty being killed or finding out she was wolf? "Either way," she muttered, "it isn't going to be easy!"

Chato finished his cigar, paid Danny for the meals, and walked out into the cold night air. He could smell the wolf in Tommy and followed the smell to a tent where he knew Tommy was sleeping. There was no doubt in his mind, Tommy was wolf and Chato was sure he didn't realize it. Leaving the camp, Chato met Scotty coming down the ridge.

"Thanks for a great time," he told his friend, slapping him on his broad shoulder as he walked by.

"See you tomorrow," Scotty replied with a big yawn. When Chato reached the cabin and went inside it was warm with light from the fireplace filling the room. He saw his mother sitting next to the fireplace, deep in thought. Removing his coat Chato went to the fire and warmed his hands.

"What did you think of Tommy?" he asked.

"I think the boy I let escape me the other night is now wolf," she replied.

"It must be from your bite and claws. I've been thinking a lot about it, and that is the only explanation I can think of."

"But how?" Tashina exclaimed.

"I don't know, we have never wounded anything before and had it get away. Do you think he will turn into the wolf with the next full moon?"

"I'm sure of it!" Tashina replied. "I'm sure of it!"

Wolf in Sheep's Clothing

Chato often had the overwhelming desire to feed, but resisted it. *They couldn't afford to be careless now,* he told himself. He knew his mother couldn't resist the wolf during the full moon and her killings alone were causing enough trouble. It wasn't long until the phase of the moon had arrived again. Tashina was up earlier than usual that morning, feeling wolf inside her start to awake. She had coffee brewed and ready before Chato woke up.

"You're up early," he said as he sat up and wiped the sleep from his eyes.

"I couldn't sleep anymore," she told him.

"I know," he said, "I can feel it too."

"I wish I could overcome it the way you can. If I could, your father would be alive today!"

"The longer I go without feeding, the harder it is for me," Chato replied. "Sometimes, just a hint of anger will bring the wolf out. Remember the plan, take the wolf as far away from camp as you can and I will go into the camps and see what happens to Tommy. If he turns wolf like we think, the camp will be in an uproar as he tries to feed. If this works out it could take some of the attention away from us as well as show us how we can spread the wolf among the camps and let them kill each other."

Tashina laughed and then snarled, saying, "When it's time, we will all feed on the camps below!" Chato laughed with her and snarled, his eyes turning yellow. About an hour before dark, Tashina and Chato left the cabin. She was trying to get as far away as she could before dark to try to keep the wolf away from the camps. Chato waved goodbye to her, heading over the ridge and into the camps to keep watch on

Tommy. It was a good thing for him to be seen during the full moon to show he wasn't a wolf. He looked for Scotty at his tent but he wasn't there, so he went to the center of town to look for Tommy. He couldn't sense Tommy anywhere and was puzzled by it. It was almost dark and the moon was already a bright orange globe in the sky. Everything was peaceful in the camp, not even a brawl going on anywhere. He was hungry and thought maybe another steak would be a good thing to chew on while he waited for things to unfold. Going to the dining tent he found a table and ordered a steak and beer from Danny. He saw the looks he got when he entered the tent and heard the whispers, although not as many as the other night.

Feeling ornery, he spoke up, "There is a full moon out tonight, boys, and here I sit eating steak instead of you!" Everyone quickly turned around and went back to eating their dinners. He wasn't sure if it was because they realized he couldn't be a wolf or if he had just scared them. It didn't take long for his steak to be ready. Famished, he eagerly dug in. He was totally engrossed in enjoying his steak when he heard a wolf howl at the outskirts of the camps. Everyone jumped up from their dinners and ran outside the tent. He took several more bites of his steak and then it howled again, this time much closer.

"It's almost quitting time," Scotty told his men as they loaded ore on the ore cart. He turned and looked back towards the entrance and saw Tommy looking into the cavern. "Finish loading the cart and we will take it out with us," Scotty told them, walking towards Tommy. Tommy stood staring into the cavern, not knowing why something was taking over his mind.

"Tommy, are you all right?" Scotty asked as he walked up.

"Huh, uh … sure, I'm okay," Tommy replied, looking confused. Scotty could see beads of sweat all over Tommy's face.

"Help them finish loading the cart and we will quit for the night," Scotty told him.

"Right, boss!" Tommy said going to the cart and helping them load the ore. As Scotty stood by the cavern opening, he felt a cold chill go up his spine.

"That place gives me the creeps," Scotty said, looking into the cavern before turning to help his miners. Looking back towards the mine entrance, Scotty could tell it was almost dark out. He had worked them longer than he had planned. When he got to the cart he could see Tommy was becoming sick, grabbing his stomach in pain.

"What's wrong?" Scotty asked as Tommy screamed out in pain and ran down the tunnel and into the cavern. "What happened?" Scotty asked his men.

"I don't know," the man replied. "He has been acting strange for about an hour now."

"Get this cart to the surface and head back to camp and I'll get Tommy and catch up to you," Scotty told them. As the miners pushed the full ore cart back to the entrance, Scotty went in the cavern after Tommy. He had just bent down and stepped inside, trying to see in the lamplight, when a terrible howl echoed throughout the cavern. Scotty was so startled his heart missed a beat and he almost fell down. In the darkness he saw two fiery yellow eyes watching him intently. Then the eyes began to come closer. Once in the lamplight, he gasped as he saw the hideous wolf-like creature standing on its hind legs, growling and showing its terrible teeth. He saw its long claws as the demon's ears laid back against its evil head. In an instant it was on all fours, growling savagely as it attacked him. He never had time to react; the wolf was on him in the second. Terrified, he felt the powerful jaws close on his shoulder and the teeth tear at his flesh. In desperation he grabbed the wolf's body and using its own momentum, threw it off him and into the mineshaft. Growling in a rage, the demon got to its feet and saw the screaming miners running for the entrance. In a second it was running after them, forgetting about Scotty.

"Run, run!" a terrified miner screamed as he saw the growling beast get thrown into the shaft. Running as fast as their legs could carry them, the miners were insane with fear. One man in the lead looked back to see the huge beast with yellow eyes catching up to them and suddenly he tripped and fell flat on his face. The others heard his bloodcurdling screams as they raced for the entrance. They were so winded now they couldn't scream as they ran for safety. The last man could hear the monster racing up behind him, growling and breathing hard as it overpowered him, savagely tearing him apart. His horrible screams were more fuel for the rest to keep running. They heard the howl again and knew the demon was still coming. Bursting out into the darkness, they ran away from the mine entrance, each going a different way. Several of the men raced towards the camps for help. The wolf howled again in the open night air at the moon shining its golden light down on the mountainside. Seeing the two miners fleeing towards the camps, the wolf went after them. Exhausted and unable to breathe, the two men stopped and tried to catch their breath. Looking back towards the mine, one of the men saw the terrible yellow eyes coming right for them.

"My God, Vernon, it's coming!" he screamed as he started to run again. Vernon looked up, and seeing the yellow eyes, ran for his life, chasing after his friend. In the moonlight Vernon could see the trail and knew their only chance was to make it to the camps.

"Run!" he screamed to his partner. "Run!" Once they crested the ridge and headed down the other side towards the camps, he knew his friend was done for.

"I can't go any farther!" the miner yelled.

"Don't stop now, we are almost there!" Vernon yelled as the miner tripped and fell. Knowing he couldn't help, Vernon ran on, hearing the terrible screams of the man who had fallen. His lungs felt as if they were bursting as he continued to drive his legs. He was at the edge of town when he collapsed, unable to run any farther. Suddenly the demon was on him. He could feel its crushing weight and its terrible teeth as it tore at his arm and chest. Suddenly it stopped and standing on its hind legs above him, howled. Frightened beyond belief, Vernon's eyes went black and closed.

The wolf saw people scurrying around the camp after it howled and ran towards them growling, eager for another meal. Entering a tent full of people it slashed out with its claws and jaws at what ever came close enough. Seeing so many people in one place the wolf attacked them all until not catching anyone it picked out one in particular and leaped on the screaming man, killing him. The tent collapsed on the wolf as it gulped down large mouthfuls of the man's flesh. Eating its fill, the wolf ripped open the tent. Still growling, it looked for its next victim.

The camp was in a blind panic. Men were running everywhere, screaming for help. Chato noticed after he left the dining tent that some men appeared to have been attacked by the creature but had gotten away.

"Good!" he mumbled out loud. "Good!" Walking towards the screaming, he came around the side of a tent and came face-to-face with the wolf. Its savage yellow eyes were glaring at him as it growled, its bloody jaws opening to show its terrible teeth. Standing on its hind legs the wolf began to walk towards him. Its lips were curled back as it growled and then stopped, sensing something about him. Dropping to all fours it raced around him and into the street beyond. Chato could see bullet holes in its body when it stood up and knew the minute it had entered the camp it had been shot. He had heard rifle shots right after he heard it howl the second time. Turning to follow the wolf, he heard a barrage of gunfire and a mournful howl, and then all was silent. Hurrying to where he had seen the wolf last, he saw a crowd gathered around a body.

"My God!" a voice declared. "It's Tommy!"

Pushing through the crowd, Chato saw Tommy's lifeless body lying in the street.

"I killed him with a silver bullet in the heart!" a small man dressed in buckskins and a fur hat exclaimed. "My God, it was Tommy all the time!"

"He killed Trevor before he came to town!" a voice exclaimed.

"Yes, Trevor must have been the one who gave Tommy the wounds on his back."

Hearing all he needed to hear, Chato left the crowd and headed back to the cabin. As he reached the outskirts of the camp he saw several people helping a man he recognized.

"Vernon is that you?" he asked the wounded man.

"Yes, it's me all right! I thought I was a goner, but for some reason the wolf just took several bites out of me and left."

"Where is Scotty?" Chato asked, now knowing why Scotty wasn't in camp.

"He's back at the mine, maybe dead for all I know," Vernon answered. "It was that kid Tommy, he turned into a wolf and tried to kill us all!" Leaving Vernon with the others Chato followed the trail back to the mine.

"Wait for a search party to be formed," a miner warned him.

"I don't know if Scotty can wait," Chato answered as he walked off in the darkness. In several places on the trail Chato found dead bodies torn to pieces. The temptation was almost overpowering for him to change and feed on them but he knew he must find out about Scotty first. Going to the mine, he went inside and found more dead bodies. Taking a lamp from a dead miner, he lit it and made his way deep into the mine. At the cavern entrance, he heard a moan and saw Scotty getting to his feet.

"Are you all right?" Chato asked. Scotty winced in pain and with rubbery legs tried to walk to Chato. "Here, let me help!" Chato told him going to his side. He could see in the lamplight Scotty's shoulder was badly torn up and he had bled heavily. Putting Scotty's good arm over his shoulder and neck, Chato got under him and helped him to the entrance of the mine. The way Scotty was bleeding he knew he would never make it to town, so Chato used his wolf strength to practically carry Scotty down to the cabin. Once inside, Chato got a fire going and cleaned Scotty's wounds. Once he put bandages on them the bleeding stopped. Scotty was in a great deal of pain while Chato was putting the bandages on his wounds and fell into a fitful sleep when he was through. Leaving the cabin, Chato listened and smelled for any sign of the search party. Hearing none, he went back up to the mountain and took advantage of all of Tommy's handiwork. He let the wolf inside him feast on as many of the dead bodies as possible, knowing no one would be the wiser. Feeding all night on the bodies, he quit when the wolf was gorged. Returning to the cabin just before dawn, he washed the blood from the feasting off in the creek. Once inside the cabin he checked on Scotty and found him to be breathing, but just barely. Scotty had lost so much blood he would have surely been dead by now if he were not wolf. Chato couldn't sense the wolf in Scotty, but he was sure that was what was keeping him alive. Feeling tired, Chato put more wood in the fireplace and then crawled in his bunk and went to sleep.

Tashina entered the cabin just before dawn after standing outside listening to the noises coming from the miner's camps over the ridge. As she opened the door she smelled blood, Scotty's blood. Fear leapt through her and she immediately thought Chato had turned and killed Scotty. She knew she was wrong the minute she walked inside. She sensed Scotty was there before she saw him. Closing the door, she saw him lying on her bed. Bewildered, she went to the bed and could hear his labored breathing and saw he was shivering in a cold sweat. She saw the bandages on his arm and shoulder and smelled the wolf on him from his attacker. "It wasn't Chato; it was Tommy!" Tommy must have turned wolf and attacked Scotty. The cabin was toasty warm yet Scotty was still shivering under the blankets. *She had to warm him*, she thought to herself, *but how?* Taking off her coat, she climbed into the bed with Scotty and wrapped her arms around him, holding him close under the blankets.

That's how Chato found them when he awoke later that morning. Tashina woke up when she heard Chato get up. Still holding Scotty, she could tell he had warmed up and was not shivering anymore. Crawling out from under the blanket, she went to the fireplace.

"What happened to him?" she asked Chato.

"Can't you tell?" Chato asked.

"Tommy?" Tashina said. Chato nodded his head, putting more wood in the fire.

"He turned wolf in the mine and attacked Scotty and then chased and killed miners all the way to the camps and more."

"Did he escape?"

Chato shook his head slowly. "He was shot with a silver bullet in the heart and killed on the spot. I saw firsthand what a silver bullet could do, and it isn't pretty! Scotty is lucky to be alive! I'm not sure why the wolf let him live. His wounds are serious and I'm sure he would have died already if he weren't starting to turn wolf." Grabbing the coffee pot he went to the creek for water. Tashina watched him go and then walking to Scotty's side, placed her hand on his shoulder, and whispered to his unconscious mind, "What am I going to do with you now?" When Chato returned with the coffee pot full of fresh water, Tashina was under the covers again next to Scotty, already asleep.

Chato made some coffee and sat at the table planning what to do next. After feeding all night he didn't want any breakfast. He could hear Scotty's labored breathing as well as his mother's steady breathing from where he sat. He decided he would go into town and see what was going on so he had a better idea of what might happen tonight. Putting on his jacket, he went out the cabin door, closing it quietly behind him. He could see the search party ride up the trail to the mine. "I might as well start there," he muttered to himself. Taking a shortcut above the cabin to the mine, he waved at the riders as he got close enough for them to see him. Walking out to meet them he said, "I found Scotty still alive last night and took him to our cabin. My mother is looking after him and it's touch and go whether or not he will make it."

"He is lucky then," a hard-looking miner said. "Everyone else has been almost completely eaten. It's the most gruesome thing I have ever seen!"

"I'm going into camp for some medical supplies," Chato told them. "I just wanted you to know about Scotty."

"Thanks," the man said. "Tell Scotty we sure hope he gets better soon. And tell him we killed the animal that attacked him and ate all of his friends."

"I'll tell him," Chato replied as he headed down the mountain towards camp. Following the trail down the mountain and past the badly-eaten bodies, he chuckled to himself. "Now I know why I'm not hungry this morning."

He went straight to the hospital tent for bandages and medicine and to see how many had been injured by the wolf. Seeing the doctor, he told him about finding Scotty and asked for bandages and whatever else he would need.

"I'm getting short on everything right now," the doctor told him. "I'm treating six wolf bite victims from last night. They say the wolf was Tommy. I can't hardly believe it, he was such a good kid."

"Well I guess it just goes to show you that you never really know," Chato replied. Going to the back of the tent, the doctor brought out a jar of salve and some clean bandages.

Chato paid for them as the doctor told him "This is all I can spare for now. If Scotty needs me, let me know and I'll be there," the doctor told Chato. "There is something about that man I really like."

Chato took the bandages and turned away smiling, muttering under his breath, "There is something about him all right, and I have a feeling you don't want to see what it is!"

As Tashina slept next to Scotty, she began to dream. She saw herself hold her hand out to Scotty, asking him to take it. In a seductive voice she said, "Take it, Scotty. I won't hurt you." Unable to resist, he reached out and took her tiny hand in his. Slowly he pulled her to him. She looked up at him with her big fawn eyes and then suddenly turned into the wolf, ready to bite. As the wolf in her looked up at Scotty it saw he had turned into a wolf also, staring down at her with fiery yellow eyes.

Startled, Tashina awoke from her dream and realized Scotty was dreaming.

"No," he muttered, "She is not a wolf …" then the dream was gone and he was resting quietly. Tashina watched him sleeping as she lay next to him. How was she going to tell him what he had become and what she had always been? She wished she knew how he would take it. She could help him if he would let her or he could be their undoing if she weren't careful.

When Chato returned to the cabin, Tashina and Scotty were still resting. Tashina heard him close the door and got up to see what he had found out. "Were many hurt by the wolf?" she asked, going to the fireplace and pouring a cup of coffee.

"A total of six is what the doctor said," Chato answered.

"That's seven with Scotty. Tommy must have been very careless."

Chato took the cup of coffee from his mother and smiled, saying, "The more the merrier if you asked me!" Laughing, Tashina poured herself a cup of coffee and then looked at Scotty lying on her bed.

"What about Scotty?" she asked.

"What about him?"

"You know what I mean. I can sense the wolf in him now. We need to warn him about what's going to happen, we owe him that much and more," she said in a concerned voice.

"He is one of us now, and will be able to sense the wolf in you when you tell him." Chato walked over to Scotty and stood by him for a moment before returning to the table. "You're right," he told her, "he's a wolf, I can feel it."

"Will he turn into the wolf tonight or wait for the new full moon a month from now?"

Chato shrugged his shoulders. "I don't know," he muttered. "We will see how he acts this afternoon.

"I'm not going to let Scotty run rampant in the camp and be shot like the others," Tashina told him in a concerned voice. "I've been worried about how to deal with Scotty and now maybe the choice has already been made."

"That's why I brought him to the cabin last night, so we can keep an eye on him and warn him of what he has become," Chato told her in a soft voice. Tashina was relieved to hear that Chato felt the same as she did about Scotty's fate.

"Let me see those bandages," she said, taking the bandages and medicine and going to Scotty's side. Pulling the blankets back she slowly removed the blood-soaked bandages covering his wounds. "Look," Tashina whispered pointing at the wounds, "they are almost healed." As Chato got closer he could see the wounds were healing at a rapid rate.

"I'm sure if he wasn't wolf, he would have bled to death last night before I found him," Chato whispered, sipping his coffee.

"I guess we can thank Tommy for something," Tashina said in a whisper as she covered Scotty back up. Following Chato back to the table Tashina whispered, "Everything is going as planned except for Scotty."

"Yes, now all we have to do is wait and see what unfolds," Chato chuckled, his eyes turning yellow.

That afternoon Scotty woke up, startled and not knowing where he was at first. Sitting up, he saw the fuzzy image of someone sitting next to him, talking softly. As his vision began to clear he saw it was Tashina, she was telling him softly he was okay and at their cabin. Tashina was relieved when Scotty recognized her and calmed down.

"What happened?" Scotty asked.

"Do you remember?" she replied

Massaging the back of his sore neck with his big hand, Scotty started to remember. "Tommy," he exclaimed. "It was Tommy! He turned into a wolf-like demon and attacked me and that's all I remember," he gasped.

"Yes, Tommy did turn into a wolf, attack you, and then followed your friends back to town, killing many of them," Chato told him in a loud voice from the table.

Scotty squinted his eyes at Chato and asked, "How did I get here?"

"Chato found you and brought you here last night," Tashina

whispered in a soft voice. Feeling dizzy and light-headed, Scotty lay back on the bed with Tashina's help. He smiled as he felt her soft hands and long hair touching him as he closed his eyes and fell back to sleep.

"Is he okay?" Chato asked.

"He is fine," Tashina answered. "Just still weak from losing so much blood." Covering him with a blanket she returned to the table, smiling at Chato. "You will need to stay with him tonight, you know that don't you?"

"I brought him here didn't I? If he takes the news of being wolf well, he will be a strong ally, almost like one of the family," he said grinning as Tashina blushed. Chato looked serious and asked, "What if he takes the news badly and doesn't want anything to do with us?"

Tashina sighed. Looking deep into Chato eyes, she said, "Then you will have to kill him before he turns wolf." Both of them turned and looked at the man who had broken down their defenses and had become their friend.

Wolf among Friends

Tashina waited until the middle of the afternoon. Scotty still wasn't awake, so she went to him and tried to wake him up. They couldn't wait any longer. If Scotty was going to turn into the wolf tonight, he needed to be aware of it before it happened or they might lose him forever with the silver bullet in his heart. "Scotty, wake up," she whispered in a gentle voice. She shook his good shoulder carefully as he opened his eyes. "How do you feel?" she asked.

He was relieved to see Tashina sitting next to him and hoped it wasn't a dream, being near her. "I feel fine," he said, sitting up.

"Do you remember how you got here?" she asked him, looking deep into his eyes.

"You told me Chato saved me from the wolf last night," he replied in a confused voice.

"That's right. Let me see how your wound is looking," she said, checking under his bandages. "They're almost all healed," she said, smiling, as she sat back down on the bed.

"They can't be," Scotty replied, "not that fast." Raising his wounded arm he discovered he could move it and his shoulder with very little pain. Lifting the bandages on his upper arm he saw the arm was almost healed. "How did you do this?" he asked Tashina in a bewildered voice.

"I didn't, you did."

"I did? What do you mean?" Then he remembered how Tommy's wounds had healed almost completely the day after the wolf had bitten him. Feeling peculiar, he got out of bed and sat next to Tashina, resting his head in his hands. "Tommy's wounds healed quickly too and look what happened to him!"

"Don't worry," Tashina said softly. "It will be all right." She placed her arm around him resting her head on his shoulder. Seeing Chato sitting at the table watching him, Scotty asked, "Was there a full moon last night?"

"Yes," Chato told him. "It was big and yellow."

"That's it then," Scotty yelled, jumping to his feet. "Tommy turned into a wolf after being bitten by a wolf. That's why I'm healing so quickly, like Tommy. I'm going to turn into a wolf either tonight or with the next full moon phase. Oh my God!" he said in shock, sitting back on the bed.

"Don't worry, Scotty, everything is going to be fine," Tashina said, looking lovely and smiling at him. Scotty saw how she looked into his eyes and felt a deeper attraction to her than he had ever felt before. He sensed something different about her but he didn't know what it was.

"Don't you see?" he told her in a worried voice. "I may turn into a wolf tonight for all I know. As much as I hate to say it, I need to go as far away from you as possible! If I do turn wolf I couldn't bear to hurt you, either of you," he said looking at Chato.

"Are you hungry Scotty?" Chato asked.

"Now that you mention it, I'm starved!"

"I'll go out and cut you a couple steaks off a fresh deer we have hanging in the trees," Chato said, opening the cabin door and shutting it behind him.

Scotty was puzzled. "Don't you understand?" he said softly to Tashina. "I may turn into a wolf and kill you before the night is over!"

"Scotty," Tashina said in a quiet voice as she got up and stood in front of him. "Do you like what you see?"

Scotty was puzzled and confused. "You know I adore you! But now that I am a wolf I have to forget all of that and accept my fate."

"Now that you are wolf, do you sense anything different about me?" she asked, looking deep into his eyes.

Scotty looked at her standing before him, "There is something different, but I can't tell what it is."

"What if I told you the wolf in you now couldn't hurt me?" she said smiling at him.

"Are you sure?"

"Yes, I'm sure. Chato and I are the last of the wolf tribe that used to live on this mountain. Our people were trapped and killed in that cavern you blasted into. Scotty," she said in a trembling voice. "We are wolf people. Do you know what I'm saying?"

Scotty looked at the beautiful woman standing before him, and suddenly realized what she was saying. "My God!" he exclaimed. "You turn into a wolf during the full moon, don't you?"

Tashina nodded her head slowly, watching Scotty to see what he would do next. Holding her hand out to him she smiled and said in a seductive voice, "Take my hand, Scotty, and join me as my mate." Looking deep into his eyes she said, "Don't be afraid, come to me, and join us." Scotty could sense the wolf in her now as she looked deep into his eyes. Unable to control his feelings, he stood up next to the bed and reaching out, took her tiny hand in his. Pulling her to him just like in the dream, he held her close and said he would never leave. As he held her close, Tashina could sense he was committed to her regardless of what might happen, and she smiled and held him even tighter.

Suddenly, the door opened and Chato entered holding two large bloody steaks. He had waited for a while outside the door while Tashina told Scotty about herself. If Scotty had taken it any other way, Chato would have entered the cabin as the wolf and killed him. "Still hungry," Chato said, "after what you just heard?"

"I'm starving," Scotty replied, releasing Tashina and seeing Chato for the first time for what he was. Chato gave the steaks to Tashina and turned to face Scotty.

"I'm glad to have you on our side," Chato said, smiling, and releasing the tension in the room. "Now get over there and eat a steak so you can get your strength back," he said, laughing as he sat at the table.

Scotty joined him and seeing the steaks in Tashina's hand still dripping blood, asked her not to cook them. "Give them to me the way they are."

"Are you sure? You usually want your meat cooked well done."

"Not anymore," he said as he started to wolf down the raw steaks. Both Tashina and Chato laughed at him as he smiled and gorged himself on the bloody steaks.

After Scotty was through eating, he sat back and saw his old friends in a totally different light. He would do anything to be at Tashina's side and was starting to believe she felt the same.

"How do you feel?" Tashina asked him.

"Great!" he said, smiling up at her.

"We are not sure if you will turn wolf tonight or not," Chato told him. Looking at Tashina he said, "Mother will, as soon as the moon is up. She will try to take the wolf in her far away, but the problem is you. I'm going to stay close to you for the next few days to see how the wolf in you reacts. If you turn wolf and go into the camps like Tommy, you will be killed with a silver bullet, and mother doesn't want that," he said, smiling at her. "Six others were attacked by the wolf and lived. When they turn wolf they will run wild in the camp, spreading the wolf among the others. Soon the wolves will drive everyone from the mountain."

"That's what you want, isn't it?" Scotty asked.

"We brought you and the miners here to help us break into the cavern that trapped our people long ago," Chato told him.

"With our people set free, we hoped to drive everyone away and be like we once were," Tashina said in a soft voice. "But then you broke into the cavern we found all our people were long dead. When Tommy escaped from me and healed so quickly, we discovered another way to drive everyone from this mountain."

"You are the one who attacked Tommy and his partner?" Scotty asked in a disbelieving voice.

"Yes," Tashina replied. "It was the wolf inside me!"

"So the plan is to drive people from the mountain by letting the wolves kill everyone?" Scotty said.

"That's it," Chato said. "It's working pretty well so far."

As the evening sun started its downward arc towards the mountaintops, Scotty began to tremble and cramp up. Stumbling to the bed, he sat there gasping in pain.

Going to his side, Tashina told him in a soft voice "The pain is your body changing, allowing the wolf to exist as your equal."

"Does this mean I will change into the wolf tonight?" he gasped in pain. Tashina could tell he was frightened by his pain and tried to soothe him.

"Don't fight your body, let the wolf take control and it will be much easier for you."

"It's not dark yet," he moaned. "Why am I changing now?"

"You are not changing yet," she told him softly. "Your body is just trying to adjust to the wolf." Tashina left Scotty and went to the table where Chato was sitting.

"You know what this means?" Chato said with a big smile. "The others will turn also and soon the camps will be running in blood." Together they both laughed as Tashina looked at Scotty.

"Take him to the mine and let him turn into the wolf there," she told him. "If he turns wolf here you won't be able to control him."

"I won't be able to control him any better at the mine," Chato replied.

"I know, but at least it's a little farther up the mountain," she said in a worried voice. "There is less than an hour left of daylight, so we had better get started."

"Maybe you should come to the mine with us," Chato said in a wondering voice. "He might follow you when you turn wolf."

Tashina stopped and thought for a moment, "Maybe you're right, let's do it!" Helping Scotty get to his feet, they took him out of the cabin and to the mine.

"Why did we come here?" Scotty asked. Looking up at the sun hiding behind the mountaintops, Chato knew it would be dark in just a few minutes.

"Take him into the cavern and stay with him until you turn wolf," he told his mother. "If he turns first, I will try to slow him up until you join him." Quickly Tashina helped Scotty go deeper and deeper into the mine.

"We will need a lamp," Scotty groaned as they walked into the darkness.

"Look with your eyes," Tashina whispered.

Scotty looked in the darkness and was amazed. He could see perfectly all the way to the end of the tunnel. Once at the cavern, Tashina helped Scotty inside. "Let's go in to the cavern as far as we can," Tashina told him in a whisper, feeling her body starting to change. They made it to the far end of the cavern before Tashina, overcome by pain, dropped Scotty and fell to her knees in the cool earth. Scotty stumbled and unable to move his legs, fell on his side to the ground. Looking up he saw Tashina's lovely body starting to transform. Her eyes were a fiery yellow as her face contorted and twisted until the face of the snarling wolf appeared. He saw her slender arms and small hands burst into the hairy arms and claws of the wolf. Her beautiful legs twisted and bent, bursting with fur and paws as she both groaned and snarled in pain. Trying to stand, her body twisted and snapped, causing her to scream as her chest burst into the wide, hairy chest of the wolf. She screamed again for a moment, and then the scream was choked off by a hideous howl that shook the air in the cavern. Scotty was petrified, frozen in fear from seeing his wonderful Tashina change like that.

He was in so much pain now, his eyes were blurry and he felt as if his flesh was being torn from his face. He felt fur and large teeth emerge on his face as he screamed in pain. Looking at his hands clenched in agony, he saw them burst apart and change into hairy hands with long claws. Blind now from the pain, he twisted and screamed, feeling as if his legs were first on fire and then being pulled off. His chest and his back seemed to be crushed as he screamed again through the mouth of the wolf. He heard himself growl savagely as he fought back the pain. Suddenly the pain was gone and he could see he was standing up. And then the wolf he had become raised its head and uttered a terrible howl. Seeing through the wolf's eyes now, he saw the wolf Tashina had become on all fours, snarling and growling at him. He heard the wolf inside him snarl and growl back, as his mind was taken over by the wolf.

Chato waited at the entrance of the mineshaft as Tashina took Scotty into the cavern. Looking behind him on the mountainside Chato saw the last rays of sunshine were gone and darkness was starting to creep across the mountain. The moon was bright and orange again, already climbing into the sky. He felt the wolf's powerful urge as he looked at the moon. The wolf inside him was growling, eager to come out. Resisting the temptation, he turned away and looked down into the dark mineshaft. He only waited a few minutes more when he heard the savage howl of his mother. He had heard that howl all his life. He wouldn't be able to stop her or slow her down if she came out without Scotty. The wolf in her was too strong to listen to him. Then he heard another deeper, louder howl and knew it had to be Scotty. He could see down the dark shaft and saw one wolf leap out of the cavern and stand, looking confused. Then another, larger wolf followed. Tashina howled savagely again and then ran towards Chato and the entrance. Chato stepped back away from the entrance and waited. When his mother got to the entrance she stopped, growling and snarling at him. The wolf in Scotty suddenly burst from the entrance, growling when it saw Chato. Snarling, it curled its lips, showing its terrible teeth. Chato felt their yellow eyes probing his very soul. Suddenly, Tashina ran into the night towards the top of the mountain. Scotty turned and watched her go. Growling, he stood up, howled and then ran headlong after her.

"Perfect!" Chato exclaimed in happiness. "Perfect!" He knew it was important for his mother to take the wolf in her and Scotty as far away as possible. Able to do it thus far, Chato doubted she could do it all night long. Leaving the mine he hurried down the mountain towards the camps. He could already hear gunshots and the night was just getting starting.

Vengeance of the Wolves

Vernon was surprised that morning when the doctor told him he was almost completely healed from the wolf attack the night before.

"I might as well remove these bandages completely," the doctor exclaimed. "They are not doing anything for you now." As the doctor removed the bandages he said, "Everyone who was attacked by the wolf and lived has healed like this. I've only seen one person heal this quickly before."

"Oh yeah, who was that?" Vernon asked.

The doctor started to say Tommy, but then decided not to. There wasn't any sense scaring Vernon by telling him the wolf that attacked him had healed quickly also. "I can't remember his name," the doctor replied. "It was a long time ago." Seeing the doctor was finished removing his bandages, Vernon sat up and moved his arms and shoulders carefully. *The doctor was right*, he thought to himself, *he only felt a little stiff.*

"You said six others were attacked last night too."

"Yes, several have left this morning already healed. Their wounds were not as serious as yours."

Standing, Vernon took a deep breath and told the doctor "I feel fine, better than I have for a long time. How much do I owe you, doc?" he asked.

"A couple of dollars ought to cover it," the doctor replied. Paying him, Vernon walked out of the tent feeling like a new man. He had more energy than he had since he was a young boy. Starving, he went to the dining tent and finding it almost empty, sat down at one of the tables. Danny greeted him saying he was early.

"I'm starving!" he pleaded. "I can't wait to chew on one of your delicious steaks. Feed me now or I will go to the corrals and kill one of your beef for myself," he kidded.

"All right, all right!" Danny said bringing him a mug of coffee.

"Coffee?" Vernon said looking at the steaming cup.

"Yes coffee," Danny replied. "It's too early for beer, even for you. Let's see, you are a medium rare customer aren't you?"

"I was until this morning, but now I want my steak as bloody as you could make it."

"Do you want it raw?" Danny asked, smiling

"No, not raw, but not much more than brown on the outside."

"I call that bloody rare," Danny said in a puzzled voice. "And you are the fourth one this morning ordering bloody steaks. What's the world coming to?" he muttered, as he went back to the grill. While Vernon sat drinking his coffee, he noticed some people seemed to be pulling out. As Danny refilled his cup, he pointed to the streets saying, "People are leaving right and left, is there another strike somewhere?"

"It's the wolf, it's got everyone scared after last night's attacks."

"I thought the wolf was killed last night for good!" Vernon said.

"It was," Danny replied filling his coffee cup. "But some people are not sure and don't want to tempt fate."

As Vernon watched the busy street with so many people leaving he muttered, "At this rate no one will be left to buy your steaks by nightfall."

"Yeah, yeah," Danny said, grinning as he left the table. It wasn't long until Danny returned with Vernon's steak. "It's almost a waste to fire my grill up to cook something this rare," Danny told him as he sat the thick steak on the table.

"Just right," Vernon said, looking at the blood around the edges of the plate.

"Doesn't anyone appreciate a well-cooked steak anymore?" Danny muttered, leaving Vernon to enjoy his steak. As Vernon ate the steak he was amazed at how much he enjoyed the blood in the meat. After eating, Vernon saw a wagon loaded with pine coffins drive slowly by. Walking behind the wagon were several friends helping a grieving sister follow her brother's coffin to the makeshift cemetery. Her brother was his best friend Dave. The wolf had killed Dave just before it jumped on him. He felt goose bumps on his arms as he thought about the wolf tearing at his body. He could hear her sobbing even from the dinning tent and it tore him up inside. She was once his girlfriend and was very dear to him. They were going to get married, until one day she saw a rich banker and told him he wasn't good enough for her any more. Joining the grieving crowd, he offered his condolences to the others, when she saw him and ran into his arms.

"Mary, I'm so sorry about Dave!" he told her in a broken voice.

"I know," she said kissing his cheek. "I know!" Holding him tightly she whispered, "I thought you were dead!"

"No, only cut up a little that's all," he replied softly in her ear. Seeing everyone standing around them, Vernon held her and looking into her eyes, told her, "We have to take care of Dave now, Mary." Nodding, she held him close as they walked quickly behind the wagon to catch up.

After the funeral was over, Vernon helped Mary walk back to town. Mary's tears were drying up and as she smiled, Vernon saw she was still as beautiful as ever.

"Have you thought about what you will do now?" he asked her.

"No, with Dave gone I'm alone," she whimpered, sobbing softly on his shoulder.

"You aren't alone," he told her.

"I'm not?"

"No, not when you have me, if you want me."

"Of course I want you," she told him, leaping into his arms. As he took her home he was overcome with joy. He had his Mary back and nothing would take her away again. Their love had been rekindled, and they spent the rest of the day in her tent.

As the light in the tent began to fade with the setting sun, Mary whispered in his ear, "I love you." Smiling he turned to her and started to reply when he curled up in pain, holding his stomach. He groaned and cried out in pain as she asked, "What is it, what is the matter?" in a frightened voice.

"Nothing," he said, sitting up. "I'm okay." Sitting at the edge of the bed he felt better. Getting dressed, he told her, "I need to go out and get some fresh air, don't worry I'll be okay. My stomach's just upset from eating a raw steak earlier."

"No wonder you don't feel good," she replied. Getting out of the bed, she put a robe on and started building a fire in the wood stove. "Get some fresh air, and when you get back I will have some hot stew for you to eat. I've got a whole pot I made for Dave, sitting right here." Vernon felt weird; he could hear everything going on outside the tent. It was like he was already outside. Standing, he walked slowly past her, smiling and winking at her as he opened the tent flap and walked outside. Once outside the tent, he breathed in deep the evening air. Beads of sweat were scattered across his forehead. Wiping his forehead with his arm, he realized he had forgotten his wool cap inside the tent. He was a small man only a little over five feet five inches tall and barely weighed one hundred and fifty pounds. Dressed in leather boots almost to his knees, he wore a heavy wool shirt tucked into his canvas pants. Suspenders held his pants up as well as a wide leather belt. His pants were tucked into the tops of his tall boots. The shirt he wore had holes worn all over it and was the only thing he could find after the wolf tore his best shirt up. Short black hair uncombed and unruly covered his head, contrasting with his blue eyes.

Severe stomach pains engulfed his body as he gasped in pain and ran doubled over behind the tent. Dropping to his knees, he tried to vomit, but couldn't. He could hear Mary filling a lamp and lighting it, as he fought back his stomach pains. The lamplight caused the tent to glow inside and he could see Mary's shadow on the tent wall. The cool night breeze blew gently on his face as darkness swept across the mountain. Gasping for breath, he looked up at the brilliant orange moon and felt dizzy, falling back to the ground. As his vision began to get blurry, his head felt as if it was splitting apart. Fighting the pain, he groaned and twisted in the dirt. Unable to stand the pain any longer he screamed through a throat he realized wasn't his own. Thrashing in pain, he rolled against the side of the tent. Mary was just getting the stew on the stove to warm up when she heard a whimper at the back of the tent. Going to the tent wall she listened and heard moaning and groaning.

"Vernon is that you?" she asked in a whisper. Hearing no reply, she could still hear the sound of someone suffering terribly. "Vernon are you all right?" she said in a loud voice, starting to become worried. The groaning stopped for a moment and then started again, along with thrashing and violent banging on the ground. Frightened, she stepped

123

back and heard a scream just outside the tent. Suddenly something rolled against the side of the tent, thrashing and growling. Covering her mouth with her cupped hands in fear, she screamed. Terrified, she watched the animal thrash violently on the ground against the side of the tent. She heard a man scream in pain, and she saw a hand slip under the tent. Gasping in fear she screamed again when she saw the hand was not human and had long, terrible claws. The hand reached up and ripped the side of the tent wall open. Mary heard a savage growl and then saw a hideous beast with fiery yellow eyes glaring at her. Snarling and snapping its jaws full of teeth, she saw it coming through the opening. Frozen in fear, her eyes rolled back in her head and she fainted, collapsing on the ground next to the stove. Savagely the wolf tore open the tent wall and leaped inside. Grabbing her by her shoulders it picked her unconscious body up in the air. Something deep inside the wolf screamed, "No!" and it laid her back on the ground. With a deep growl, it dropped to all fours and ran into the street. Stopping in the middle of the street, it stood on its hind legs and let out a death-defying howl. People screamed and ran everywhere. Gunfire echoed throughout the camp. The wolf saw a man point a rifle at it and felt the bullet hit its side. In a rage, it growled and charged the man. He frantically tried to load another cartridge in his rifle and then the wolf was on him. His rifle went flying as the wolf grabbed him by his throat and lifted him in the air. Screaming and kicking the man saw the wolf's terrible eyes inches from his own. Savagely, the wolf tore his head off, gulping down the spurting blood and warm flesh.

As Chato reached the ridge overlooking the camps he could see it was in a total uproar. He could see lamplights running everywhere as well as several fires broke out. Screaming and yelling people were everywhere. Gunshots echoed across the valley, along with the savage howls of the demon wolves. Chato laughed out loud at the terror spreading through the camps below. Sitting on a rock he decided to watch the camps burn from where he was. Smiling, he licked his lips. He hoped maybe a straggler would come his way. Watching the camp he saw several wolves chasing victims out into the darkness.

"Well, at least the silver bullets aren't getting everyone," he said with a chuckle. Hearing something, he looked down the trail and saw what looked like a woman running towards him. He watched her as she ran away from the danger below. He could see she was dressed in very few clothes and was barefoot. Waiting until she was almost to him, he stood up and said in a calm voice, "You're traveling fast for a woman who's barefoot." Startled, the woman screamed and started to run away. "Wait, wait, I won't hurt you!" he yelled. Hearing his voice, the frightened woman stopped, not knowing what to do. "Come on back!" he yelled to her. "Before the wolves find us." Remembering the wolves, the woman ran back up the trail to him.

"Help me!" she cried as she reached him.

"I will, I will!" he said reaching out and taking her hand. "We have to get off this trail or they will find us!" he exclaimed leading her away. Trusting him, she followed him down the side of the ridge. "Careful," he told her. "Watch where you step." Finding a place to hide, Chato had her sit down while he pretended to stand guard. He saw she was both shaking from the cold and trembling with fear. He recognized her now as she sat quietly watching him. She had long brown hair that cascaded off her shoulders and across her chest. She was one of the prostitutes who operated in the camp below. More than once he had seen her taking men into her tent. As the moonlight escaped from behind a cloud, he saw she was pretty. In the darkness, far below them a wolf howled. Immediately she jumped up and ran to his side, holding him tightly.

"Please don't let it get me!" she exclaimed in fear.

"Nothing out there is going to get you," he told her in a soft, wicked voice. Sitting down with her still hanging on to him he asked, "What is your name?"

"Molly," she replied, holding him close for both warmth and protection. He could feel her shivering as he put his arm around her.

"Don't worry," he whispered. "Everything will work out fine."

"Thank you," she replied in a whisper, "for everything you have done for me. I feel safe in your strong arms," she said seductively as she buried her head against his chest. *He is so warm*, she thought to herself, *and he seems to be getting warmer all the time.* She felt his body stiffen and twist in her grasp. *He must be watching our back trail*, she thought, clutching him tightly. She could hear his heart beating so loudly it pounded against his chest and then suddenly his chest turned into fur. Lifting her head, she stared into the fiery yellow eyes of a hideous wolf creature. Releasing him, she started to scream as the wolf tore her body apart. After gulping down several large mouthfuls of flesh, the wolf howled at the moon high above.

Chato let the wolf gorge itself on the woman, eating everything but her hair, skull, and some bones. When the wolf was through, he headed back towards the cabin. Tomorrow he would go into the camp below and see what damage had been done. Once at the cabin, he went to the creek and bathed, washing the dried blood from his body. Shivering, he went inside and lit a fire in the fireplace. Wrapping a blanket around his shoulders, he tried to warm up as he waited for the fire to warm the cabin. He knew it was several hours until daylight and he wouldn't expect his mother or Scotty back until then. Going to his bed, he buried himself under the blankets and fell asleep.

As the light of the pre-dawn fell over the mountain, Tashina started walking towards the cabin. She looked for Scotty but couldn't find him. They had found a herd of deer and that's the last time she remembered the wolf in him being near. *I hope that things went well in the camps last night*, she thought as she walked faster, eager to get out of the cold.

Scotty awoke and found himself covered in blood, sitting next to what used to be a man. All the flesh was gone from the man's bones and blood was everywhere. Gasping in shock, Scotty tasted the man's flesh on his lips. What shocked him even more was the fact that the liked the taste.

"My God!" he muttered. "What have I done?" Getting to his feet, he headed back to the cabin. He could sense where the cabin was without even thinking about it. "Where I find the cabin, I'll find Tashina," he muttered, and that was all he needed. When he got to the ridge overlooking the cabin, he looked down and saw Tashina washing in the stream. She saw him coming and waited for him to join her.

"How was your first night as the wolf?" she asked him.

"I really don't remember much about it," he replied as he joined her.

"The more you turn wolf, the more you will remember and be able to slightly control it," she told him in a soft voice. She helped him wash all the blood off and then they both ran towards the cabin to get warm. Running inside they found the cabin toasty warm.

Chato woke up and smiled at them saying, "Keep it down, I need my beauty sleep!" Laughing and yawning, Tashina went to bed, covering up with several blankets. Scotty was unsure what to do as he added more wood to the fire.

"Come to bed!" Tashina giggled, holding her covers up. Happily Scotty joined her, and curling up next to each other, they both fell fast asleep.

After resting until mid-morning, Chato woke his mother and Scotty. "It's time for us to go to the camps and see how much damage was done." Tashina got up quickly and started getting ready. Scotty was slower to rise and sat up yawning and rubbing his eyes.

"Why do we need to go into the camps?" he asked.

"We need to know how the camps are holding up and if the wolves hurt very many people," Tashina told him.

"Our plan is for us to follow the people leaving the mountain and kill them when it gets dark," Chato said, smiling.

"We will let the other wolves continue to feed in the camps while we slaughter those who flee," Tashina explained. "We will purposely wound some of the people fleeing and let them take the wolf off the mountain."

Leaving the cabin, Chato went out to the corral and caught his horse. He had it saddled when Tashina and Scotty came outside.

"I'll ride into camp and snoop around a bit before you get there," he told them, mounting his horse and riding towards the camps.

As Tashina and Scotty followed on foot, Scotty asked, "Are you sure you want to drive everyone away?"

Looking up at him, Tashina smiled and replied, "This mountain belongs to my people and we have always driven anyone away who entered our land."

"What about the people who turn into wolves?" he asked.

"They will follow the others down into the country they know," she told him. "Eventually silver bullets will kill them all, I suppose."

"What about me? Will you drive me from here?" he asked in a worried voice.

"You are wolf people now!" she told him, glaring up at him. "You belong on this mountain with me. It's going to get messy from now on," she said as they walked up the ridge. "As the wolf, you will be killing and eating people you have known. Can you do that?" she asked.

"The wolf in me will do pretty much whatever it wishes and I can't stop it. But like you said, I belong on this mountain with you!"

Death in the Family

As soon as they could see the camps below, they were both shocked. Many of the tents were burned and those that weren't were only wooden floors and wood sides. They could see dust rolling off the side of the mountain and knew it was from a steady stream of travelers leaving the camps.

Chato rode into the camp in time to see the dining tent come down. He saw Danny and several others pull down the canvas tent and load it on a wagon. Riding up to the wagon he could see most of Danny's property was already loaded.

Chato waved to Danny and asked, "Where is everybody headed in such a hurry?"

"Anywhere besides this mountain and those damn wolves!" Danny replied. "I almost lost my life last night!" he said in an excited voice. Lifting his arm he showed Chato it was bandaged from his bicep to his elbow. "Damn wolf took a bite out of my arm on the way by, but I was one of the lucky ones. More than a few lost their lives last night."

"How many wolves were there?" Chato asked.

"I only saw the one, but from the sounds of it there must have been many more. You would be wise to come out with us," Danny told Chato. "As soon as the camps are empty the wolves will scour the mountain for food. Get your mother and get out of here while you still can!" Danny yelled as he turned to gather more of his belongings.

As Chato rode down the makeshift street, he felt people watching him and heard them say he was one of the owners who had lived here all his life. Quickly he moved along, almost wishing he hadn't ridden into the camp. Then he sensed a wolf in front of him. What he saw was a young man loading a stove in the back of a small wagon. It was Vernon. Vernon had told him about Scotty still being back at the mine when Tommy ran rampant. He knew the young man had turned wolf last night, killing his friends. Chato waved at him and smiled, knowing he had lived through his first night as the wolf. Vernon saw Chato waving at him and waved back as he loaded the wagon. As Chato rode by he saw a nice-looking young lady folding blankets and packing them away in a trunk.

He heard her yell, "Vernon the trunk is ready to be loaded."

"Okay Mary," he replied. "I'll be right there." As Chato rode through what was left of the camp, he saw several people with bandages covering wounds he guessed came from wolf attacks. Watching the people streaming down the mountain road, he grinned and almost laughed at what awaited many of them tonight.

As Tashina and Scotty walked down the ridge to camp, they were amazed at how fast the camp was leaving. Almost to the camp, they saw a group of four hunters ride by. Suddenly, one hunter dressed in buckskins jerked his horse around and rode hard towards them. Skidding his pony to a halt, he jumped nimbly to the ground and pointed his rifle at Tashina. Scotty recognized the man as Tyler, the man he had met in the saloon that told everyone about the wolf legend.

"You're the cause of all this!" Tyler yelled, pointing his rifle at Tashina. "The legend is right, you are wolf people on this mountain and now you have spread into the rest of us!" Scotty could tell that Tyler was dead serious.

Holding his big hand up, he said, "Now take it easy, Tyler, this woman never hurt anyone."

"Yeah right!" Tyler snarled. "I had to shoot a good friend of mine last night because of her."

"You don't mean that," Scotty replied. "You're just hurt and confused."

"I told you I liked you, Scotty, and I do, but this woman has cast a spell on you. Can't you see her for what she really is? I've got a silver bullet for you, aimed at your evil heart!" Tyler yelled at Tashina in an angry voice. "You know what silver does to the likes of you, don't you?" he sneered. Cocking his rifle he started to pull the trigger when Scotty jumped in front of Tashina. "Damn it, Scotty, move, or I'll shoot you first!" Tyler yelled. "I've got a rifle full of silver bullets here and I won't hesitate to drop you with one in order to get to her."

Tashina glared at the man as Scotty muttered, "Stay behind me!" Slowly, he walked towards Tyler. "This whole thing is just your imagination," he said.

"Just my imagination! For God's sakes, man, look around you, you have been in the mine too long! People are dying every night from her kind lurking around!" Scotty slowly walked to within twenty yards when Tyler yelled, "That's close enough! This is your last chance, Scotty, you're either with her or against her. Now what will it be?"

"I won't let you shoot her," Scotty told him in a deep voice.

"You were warned!" Tyler exclaimed as he shot Scotty in the chest.

Hearing the gunshot, Chato looked in the direction it had come from just in time to see Scotty fall to his knees and then stand up again, shielding his mother from the rifleman. Kicking his pony into a dead run, he charged as the man shot again, this time knocking Scotty down. He saw his mother shield Scotty's body with her own as the rifleman aimed again.

Sensing the rider bearing down on him, Tyler whirled and fired just as the horse knocked him flying. The shot hit Chato in the shoulder but never fazed him as he leapt from his pony on the downed man. He was in a rage, drawing his knife while pinning the man to the ground. "Looking for me?" he asked in a snarl. "Or were you looking for this?" Chato's eyes turned fiery yellow only inches from the man's face as he shoved his knife deep into the man's abdomen, slicing for his heart. Seeing the man squirm and scream in pain, he pressed his face against the man's face and whispered in his ear, "Tonight I will eat you like the pig you are." He saw the fear in the man's eyes and then they went blank. Sitting up, still in a rage, he patted the man lightly on the cheek, saying "Save me a place for supper tonight!" Snarling, he stood up holding his bloody knife, and dared the others to interfere. Watching Tyler trying to kill the woman, and then get killed himself, the riders turned their ponies in disgust and rode away.

Chato saw his mother crying over Scotty and ran to her side. "He saved me!" Tashina cried. "He took two silver bullets without fear to protect me!" Chato ripped open Scotty's shirt and saw that both bullets had hit him in his chest. Pressing his ear to Scotty's chest he listened for a heartbeat. Hearing nothing, he sat up and shook his head slowly at Tashina who was cradling Scotty's head in her lap. Seeing Chato shake his head, Tashina leaned over Scotty, sobbing, and held his head tenderly. Her long hair cascaded off her shoulders and hid her grief-stricken face. Chato felt frustrated. He could see his mother in pain and couldn't do anything about it.

Looking at Tyler's body, he began to fill with rage, his eyes turning fiery yellow. Fighting to keep the wolf back, he sensed something he had not felt before. Regaining himself, he reached out and touched his mother's shoulder. Lifting her head, she pulled the hair back out of her face and stared at him, teary-eyed.

"Mother, I sense the wolf in Scotty is still alive!" he exclaimed. "Can't you feel it?" Seeing the hope in Chato's eyes, Tashina quickly wiped the tears from her eyes and concentrated on Scotty.

Suddenly her eyes lit up and she blurted out, "I can feel it too!" Laying her hand on Scotty chest she gasped, "He's not breathing, but I can feel the wolf inside him. How can this be?" she asked, pointing at the bullet holes in his chest.

"The bullets didn't hit his heart!" Chato exclaimed.

"If the wolf is still in him, he will come back to us!" Tashina almost screamed in happiness. Suddenly Scotty's eyelids fluttered for just a second. Both Tashina and Chato saw his eyes flutter and were elated.

"We need to get him back to the cabin," Tashina said in an anxious voice. Standing, Chato looked around briefly, and then catching his horse rode to the corrals and dragged back two long corral poles. They quickly fashioned them into a makeshift travois and took Scotty back to the cabin. Once inside, Tashina removed his bloody clothes and cleaned his wounds. Placing her head on Scotty's chest, she could now hear a faint heartbeat. "He is coming back to us," she said, smiling at Chato. Covering him with blankets she went to the fireplace and soon had a warm fire going.

"That was too close for comfort!" Chato exclaimed as Tashina sat down at the table with him.

Sighing, she nodded her head in agreement. "Soon the mountain will be ours again," she replied.

"You mean yours," he told her.

Startled, she looked at him saying, "I mean yours, mine, and his," pointing at Scotty.

"I've decided to leave this place," Chato told her in a calm voice. "You don't need me here now that you have Scotty." Tashina knew what he was saying was true. Chato had the power to go anywhere he wanted and still control the wolf inside him. He had only stayed on the mountain this long because of her. They hoped that when their people were free, he would find someone to be close with, but now that was not going to happen.

She looked sadly into his eyes, saying, "I will miss you, but I understand. When will you leave us?" she asked.

"I'm going to leave as soon as I know Scotty is okay," he answered. "I will return from time to time to see how you're doing and to help if you need me. I'm going to spread the wolf into the country below and enjoy watching the outcome. When I rode through the camps today I felt the presence of the wolf in several men and saw many that were wounded from the night before. Those people don't realize it now, but many of them will die tonight and others will be injured and continue taking the wolf down the mountain. There are only several more days of the full moon left and then the wolf will lie dormant, not reappearing until those people are far away."

Tashina smiled and said, "We will feed on them until they are gone from the mountain, and then you will travel with them, feeding at will, wherever they go." They laughed at how easy it would be for Chato to follow his prey.

"Tell Scotty to continue to mine the silver and I will see to it that our partner, Sam Jenkins, continues to work with us however we would like him to," he said, smiling. Snarling he said, "I'll make sure he understands our situation and is so terrified of us, he will never betray us! I will have him send supplies and haul the silver out, allowing him to make some profit, of course," he said with a wicked laugh.

"Of course," Tashina replied, laughing with him. They discussed their plans and soon found it was late afternoon. Tashina went to Scotty's bed. Removing his blankets, she checked his wounds and saw they were healing nicely. Chato moved his arm and felt that it was almost healed. Tashina laid her hand on Scotty's chest and could feel his heart beating strongly. Feeling her touch him, Scotty opened his eyes and smiled. Looking confused he suddenly remembered what had happened and sat up. Looking at his chest he saw that the bullet wounds were almost completely healed.

"I'm not dead!" he exclaimed as he jumped out of bed and stood wobbly on his feet.

"You must sit down and rest," Tashina told him in a gentle voice, helping him sit on the edge of the bed. Taking a blanket, she placed it over his back and shoulders to keep him warm.

"What about Tyler?" he exclaimed in an angry voice.

"Tyler is no more!" Chato said in a sneering voice.

"Good!" Scotty exclaimed. "And from the looks of it," glancing at the bullet holes in his chest, "I almost was no more too."

"You were very lucky the silver never found your heart," Tashina told him in a serious tone.

"Are you okay?" Scotty asked Tashina.

"I'm fine, thanks to you."

Together Chato and Tashina spent the rest of the afternoon until just before dark telling Scotty of their plans and of Chato's leaving. As the sun slowly disappeared behind the mountaintops, Chato could tell the full moon high in the sky was beginning to affect his mother and Scotty.

"It's time!" Tashina said, grabbing Scotty and taking him outside. Hurrying away from the cabin, she yelled back at Chato, "Be safe my son and remember, we are forever so our time apart will seem brief." Chato watched them disappear into the timber as darkness started to settle across the mountain. He decided he would join what was left of the travelers fleeing down the mountain tomorrow. Tonight he had a dinner date and couldn't wait to get to the main course. He smacked his lips with anticipation. Walking towards the deserted camps, he laughed a wicked laugh and said, "Tyler, I hope you never let supper get cold."

Once Vernon got their wagon loaded, he helped Mary get up on the seat. "Hurry, Vernon," she told him, "Everyone is leaving, and I don't want to be last. After last night, I never want to see this place again!"

"All right Mary, all right!" he said, climbing into the seat beside her and urging the team on.

As the wagon creaked, popped, and started to move, Vernon thought about Chato. He could tell Chato knew what he had become, and it scared him. He hoped it was only a terrible dream and that he was not the monster who had killed his friends last night. Every time he thought of it he felt nauseous and sick to his stomach. He found himself lying far back in the timber that morning, shivering in the cold. Finding his way back to camp, he found Mary terribly shaken in their badly-torn tent. She told him that a wolf had ripped open the back of the tent and entered. As it grabbed her she fainted and didn't wake until hours later. Driving the wagon down the mountain he fought back tears, knowing he was the monster who tore into her tent. If he was the wolf, he told himself, he must stop himself from hurting Mary or anyone else. Weeks ago he had been given a silver bullet by a friend and at the time he thought it was a joke. The bullet, he was told, would kill the wolf demon if you shot it in the heart. He kept the bullet thinking he would sell it for its silver value, never dreaming he might need it for himself. As they bounced along in the wagon down the rough road, he tried to convince himself he was fine but knew it wasn't true.

Mary watched Vernon as they drove away and saw he was sad having to leave this place. She wasn't, she told herself. She never wanted to be anywhere the monster was again. Shuddering, she could still see the hideous yellow eyes and large teeth. Holding her shoulders and arms she remembered the wolf tearing through the back of the tent before she fainted. When she awoke, she found herself lying next to the stove unharmed, without even a scratch. She shuddered again, as she thought about how lucky she had been.

The rest of the morning and early afternoon they traveled down the mountain in the bouncing wagon, hardly speaking to each other. Late that afternoon, Vernon decided to stop and set up camp for the night. He could tell Mary was tired and weary of the constant bouncing and rattling of the wagon. They found a place to camp next to a small stream where several other wagons had already stopped. Mary visited the other camps when she saw they were all friends of theirs. Going back to her wagon, she helped Vernon set up a tarp, making a lean-to tent off the side of the wagon

"Vernon, I visited the Gardner's and the Smith's camps while you were busy taking care of the team. They invited us to join them for supper."

"I was hoping that was them," he told her. Grabbing his rifle from under the wagon seat, he removed the silver bullet from his pocket and inserted it into the rifle. Mary knew he was worried about the wolves, knowing they were still on the mountain. "That food smells great," Vernon told her, sniffing the air.

"I can't smell anything," Mary told him, smiling.

"You can't?" He said in a disbelieving voice. "I can smell salt pork, beans, and biscuits."

"Yeah sure," she said, smiling up at him. Taking him by his arm, she pulled him towards the neighbors. He was amazed she couldn't smell the cooking as he followed her. He could even smell strong perfume on one of the women. As they walked up to the neighboring camp, Vernon saw two men with rifles handy, eating their supper. Two women were busy preparing the food as they joined them at the fire.

"Hope you're hungry," one woman said, handing Vernon a heaping plate of food. Mary's mouth dropped open when she saw what was on his plate. Exactly what Vernon had said he smelled. Vernon looked at her as he sat down, pointing at his plate and smiling.

"Was the road rough enough for you today?" one of the men sitting across the fire asked Vernon.

He nodded his head as Mary said, "It was way rougher than I remembered!" Vernon watched both men smile, and then continue eating. He had worked with both men in the mine. Zack Gardner was the one who had given him the silver bullet. As the two women filled their plates and began to eat, Mary said, "What a beautiful evening." Everyone agreed as the two men sat their empty plates down and grabbing their rifles, told the women they were going to check on the stock. Zack looked at Vernon and signaled him to follow.

"Hang on and I'll join you," he said handing Mary his partially-eaten plate of food. Leading the men away from the women's hearing, Zack turned to Vernon with a worried look.

"Do you still have the silver bullet I gave you?" he asked.

"Loaded in my rifle," Vernon replied, tapping the side of his gun.

"Good! We may need it before the night is over," Zack replied in a frightened voice. "It's almost dark and the moon is already up."

"Do the silver bullets really kill the wolves like the legend says?" Vernon asked.

"It's the truth," Zack replied. "I shot a wolf attacking Merle Zerber last night, five times without any effect before I remembered my silver bullet." Vernon could see Zack was trembling as he spoke. "Just as wolf turned for me, I loaded my rifle with the bullet and shot it, aiming where I hope the heart was." Zack stopped and closed his eyes tight, trying to forget what he had seen.

"What happened?" Vernon asked impatiently.

Opening his eyes Zack looked at him, saying, "The wolf yelped and fell, thrashing on the ground, tearing at its chest with its claws. Then suddenly it stiffened and turned into a man with a bullet hole through his chest."

"So the bullets do work!" Vernon said in deep thought.

"Keep your silver bullet loaded in your rifle chamber until we are safely away from this mountain!" Zack exclaimed.

"Why?" Vernon asked. "You said you killed the wolf."

"You don't understand," Zack gasped. "The wolf I killed was just one of at least several in camp last night. Didn't you see any where you were?"

"Sure," Vernon answered quickly. "Mary and I saw one run through our tent and escape down the street."

"Do you know how lucky you were?" Zack stated in disbelief. "They are terrible killers, and to have one pass you by is unbelievably good fortune."

"A little luck never heard anyone, I guess," Vernon replied jokingly.

"Have you still got your silver bullet, Jacob?" Vernon asked the other man. Jacob Smith was a quiet man and hardly ever spoke unless spoken to.

"Yes," he replied. "I still have mine."

As the men returned to the fire, Zack whispered, "Remember, if the wolves attack tonight, come running with your bullet." Vernon smiled at the ladies at the fire and then told Mary, "We had better get back to camp and finish setting it up before dark." Saying goodnight to everyone, Mary followed Vernon back towards their wagon. They hadn't gone far when Vernon suddenly doubled up in pain.

"What's wrong?" Mary asked in a worried voice.

Groaning and holding his stomach, Vernon told her, "I just started feeling sick all of the sudden." Fighting back the pain, he stood upright and forced himself to walk back to the wagon. The sun was down now and he could feel his body giving in to the monster inside him.

"Mary, go get Zack!" he screamed. "Hurry Mary, hurry!" Falling to the ground he doubled up again, holding his stomach. Mary ran to Zack's fire and screamed that Vernon needed him. Grabbing his rifle, Zack told the women to stay there as he yelled for Jacob. Mary was worried Vernon was having a heart attack so she ignored Zack's orders and followed him. As Zack ran up to the wagon ready to help Vernon fight the wolf, he saw Vernon withering in terrible pain on the ground. Dropping his rifle, he ran to Vernon's side.

"Get away! Get away!" Vernon gasped. "My rifle, take my rifle!" he screamed. Zack picked up his rifle unsure of what Vernon wanted. "Shoot me!" Vernon screamed in a shrill voice. "Shoot me!"

"What!" Zack gasped.

"Shoot me!" Vernon said in a deeper voice. Suddenly his eyes turned yellow and he roared, "Shoot me!" in a voice no longer his own. As Zack watched in terror, his friend's face turned into a wolf.

"My God!" he gasped as he leaped back and aimed the rifle. The savage growling of the wolf was terrifying, and Zack froze in fear, unable to shoot. Mary was hysterical and started screaming at the top of her lungs. Zack was frozen in fear and then suddenly ejected the silver bullet from the rifle and levering another cartridge into the chamber, fired at the wolf when it started to stand. The bullet hit the wolf in its chest but never stopped it as it stood on its hind legs, ready to kill and eat Zack. Mary was screaming hysterically when a blur went by her and suddenly, Jacob was standing next to Zack aiming his rifle at the wolf. In an instant he shot the wolf, knocking it to the ground. It snarled and thrashed on the ground trying to bite at the wound it in its chest. Then suddenly it was still and Vernon lay smiling in death, looking at Mary. Mary saw Vernon staring blankly at her and fainted, falling to the ground.

"I couldn't shoot! He wanted me to shoot him but I couldn't do it! Look, I even got so excited I ejected the silver bullet," Zack said, exhausted at the effort. "Thank God you came Jacob, or it would have killed us all!"

Jacob said nothing as he knelt down and picking up the silver bullet, loaded it into his rifle. They spent the rest of the night huddled together with Jacob ready with their last silver bullet. All night they heard wolf howls below them on the mountainside and prayed they wouldn't be found. Mary whimpered in shock and the women tried to comfort and help her.

"In less than one week the wolves have taken all my family!" she cried repeatedly. When the sun peeked over their horizon, casting its warm rays of sunshine across the mountainside, everyone was thankful they had lived through the night. Completely exhausted from not sleeping, they basked in the warm sunshine.

"In the daylight we are safe from wolves," Zack told them. "We must get some sleep or we will not be able to protect ourselves tonight." Nobody argued with him as they all found a place to lie down and sleep.

Leaving the Mountain

As the sun began to climb the horizon that morning, Chato got up and saddled his horse. He saw Tashina and Scotty washing at the creek when he left the cabin. As they walked up to him, he smiled saying, "I trust you both ate well last night." Tashina looked at Scotty and they both laughed.

"I can tell you after last night, no one is left in the camps," Tashina replied, licking her lips. They all laughed together, remembering the feasting they had just had.

"It's time for me to go," Chato told his mother. He could see the pain in her face as he kissed her and mounted his horse. Looking at Scotty he said, "Mine the silver and remember our plan." Scotty nodded and put his arm around Tashina. Turning his pony, Chato said, "If I tire of their flesh I will return soon. But we know that's not going to happen!" he said laughing as he prodded his pony onward.

As Tashina watched him ride away, she turned to Scotty and said, "They have come to us, and now we will go among them."

Zack and Jacob were sweating as they labored digging a shallow grave for Vernon's body. Mary was still upset and in shock as they buried Vernon, placing slabs of rock over his grave to protect it. Feeling like he needed to say something over Vernon's grave, Zack removed his hat. "Lord, this man comes to you after giving his life to protect us from the beast inside him. Lord, protect us from the beasts that surround us and show us who these animals are!" he said in a broken voice. Suddenly they heard a rider coming towards them.

Zack looked up quickly while putting on his hat and saw a rider had stopped his pony only yards away. Removing his hat, the rider said sadly, "I'm sorry for your loss. Did the wolves do this?"

"I guess you could say that," Zack replied, shielding his eyes from the bright morning sun as he studied the man.

"Would you mind if I ride along with you?" the man asked in a serious voice. "I could be of help if the wolf should return."

"You know anything about fighting these wolf demons?" Zack asked.

"Only that a silver bullet is supposed to be able to kill them," the stranger replied, reaching deep into his pocket and removing a silver bullet. "So far I haven't even seen a wolf!" the stranger exclaimed, smiling at the women.

"Sure, you can travel with us," Zack told him, "we would be glad to have you."

"Make sure tonight you have that silver bullet loaded in your rifle and not in your pocket," Jacob said in a serious voice.

"I'll do that," the stranger said, putting his hat back on his head.

"My name is Zack Gardner, this is Jacob Smith, and these lovely ladies are our wives, except for Mary whose man we just buried today."

Tipping his hat to the women the stranger said, "My name is Chato and especially to you, ma'am. I offer my services should you need them." Mary felt Chato look deep into her eyes and quickly looked away, feeling very uncomfortable.

It was midday before they got the camp packed up and began traveling down the mountain once again. Chato drove Mary's wagon for her with his horse tied behind. Mary sat in the wagon box as it bounced along, staring at Vernon's grave until she couldn't see it anymore. Every time she closed her eyes, she saw the wolf monster dying on the ground and changing slowly back into Vernon. Drying her teary eyes with a cloth, she remembered the feel of the stranger's eyes as they bore deep into her mind. *Something about him frightens me*, she thought, watching him drive the team down the mountain. Feeling exhausted, she lay down on a pile of blankets and as the wagon lumbered along, fell fast asleep.

Chato smiled to himself as he urged the team along. This was going to be easy to disappear among these travelers. He could sense no wolf in any of the party he had just joined and was surprised. They had been smart and stayed away from the bulk of the travelers last night and he knew that helped save them. *Still, something was different about Mary,* he thought to himself as he turned and looked at her sleeping in the blankets. He couldn't sense the wolf in her, but did sense something about her he couldn't identify. It puzzled him and made him even more determined to know what it was.

As they drove down the mountain, they saw campsites torn apart, blood covering everything. In most cases everyone was dead and partially if not fully eaten. Zack pushed them hard and it was almost dark when they reach the stream at the foot of the mountain. Chato unhitched Mary's team and after watering them turned them out to graze. When he returned to the wagons he saw a hungry, confused stranger appeared. The man talked to Zack, pleading with him to let him stay. As Chato walked up, the man sensed something and turned to see Chato looking into his eyes. Turning back to Zack and Jacob he pleaded, "Don't turn me away please! You don't know what it's like out there in the dark."

"All right, stay with us tonight and we can talk about traveling with us tomorrow." Looking into the evening sky, Zack said, "We better get ready, there is one more night at least of the full moon and soon it will be dark." As the women built a fire and started cooking supper, Zack went to Chato, whispering, "Watch the stranger closely as darkness falls. If he is wolf he will turn then."

Chato nodded his head and asked in a whisper, "What should I look for?"

"Just stay close to me with your silver bullet," Zack said. "And I will show you."

Chato knew the stranger was wolf the minute he entered the camp. He decided if the wolf started killing, he would let it. These people meant nothing to him. He chuckled to himself thinking about who he would feed on first and felt the wolf in him enjoy the thought. Mary was not crying as much after her long sleep in the wagon, but she still watched him closely. He couldn't tell what it was about her that made him sense something. He could tell she sensed something about him also and it puzzled her.

As darkness began to fall, Zack called all the men together behind the wagons. As the men gathered, he lifted his rifle, pointing it at both Chato and the stranger. "Take his rifle, Jacob," Zack said in a whisper.

"What's going on?" the stranger asked.

"After what I saw last night, I know we can't trust anyone until we're sure. If in a few minutes you don't turn into a wolf, you will have my deepest apologies. In the meantime these rifle barrels will point in your direction." Chato saw Jacob point his rifle at him and smiled to himself, knowing his silver bullet was still in his pocket. Suddenly the stranger screamed out in pain and doubled over, falling to the ground.

"Get away from him!" Zack yelled to Chato. Standing back, Chato watched curiously, wondering if Zack had a silver bullet in his rifle. As the stranger turned into a savage, growling wolf, Zack took careful aim at his heart and fired. Yelping in pain the wolf fell to the ground and died, turning back into the stranger. Chato sighed. He would not feed tonight unless he was the attacker. He was tempted to kill them all but decided not to. He was still curious about Mary.

The women hearing the shot screamed and ran around the wagons in time to see the wolf turn back into the stranger. Chato saw Mary gasp at the terrible sight and then look at him in fear. Smiling at his effect on her, he told her in a soft voice not to worry, he would not let anything hurt her. Confused by his piercing stare, she let him take her hand and take her back to the fire. For some reason she did feel safe when he was near her. At times when he was close, she also felt he was the only thing to fear.

Jacob followed Chato to the fire, and apologizing, gave Chato his rifle. "By the way," Chato told him with a giggle as he held this silver bullet up, "I forgot to load it."

"Oh my God!" Jacob replied. "It's a good thing we didn't need a second shot." After the women had gone back to cooking and things had settled down some, Mary brought Chato a heaping plate of food. Chato was surprised and took the plate, thanking her. "This is unexpected," he said.

"Why is that?" Mary replied.

"I never thought you liked me," he told her in a soft voice.

"I have been through so much this last week, I feel as if I'm empty inside," she told him in a whisper. Turning to return to the fire, she looked deep into his eyes, saying, "You're different that's for sure, but I don't dislike you." He watched her walk away, sensing something about her but not knowing what it was.

After eating, Chato joined Zack and Jacob, bringing in the horses for the night. He could feel Mary watching him all evening as he sat at the end of the wagons and stood guard. Around midnight, when the moon was still high, Zack came to him and asked, "How are you holding up?"

"I'm fine," Chato replied with a yawn.

"Jacob and I are going to try and get some sleep. We will relieve you in a couple hours."

"Sounds good," Chato replied. "See you in a couple hours." Chato watched Zack walk back to his wagon and check on his wife and the others. He chuckled to himself when he thought about who these travelers had watching out for them. He was tempted to feed on the stranger they had killed earlier that evening. He looked at everyone sleeping around the fire and wondered why he didn't just kill them now and feed the rest of the night.

He saw Mary had her eyes shut, sleeping soundly. He still couldn't tell what it was about her that bothered him so much. Looking into the darkness he heard a howl far out on the plains, and knew it was a wolf like himself. He wanted to feed on the stranger but resisted his hunger, as the bright moonlight lit up the night sky. Hearing the howl again, he felt his body wanting to turn into the wolf. Fighting the urge, his eyes turned fiery yellow for a second before he was himself again. Looking back towards the campfire he saw Mary was watching him again. He looked deep into her eyes but at this distance couldn't tell if she had seen his yellow eyes or not. She sat huddled against the side of a wagon wheel, wrapped in blankets. He almost wished she had seen him and would sound the alarm. It would be the excuse the wolf in him was desperately looking for. As she watched him, she suddenly got to her feet with a blanket still around her shoulders and walked quickly to him. Chato sat his rifle down, not knowing what to expect.

"Is something wrong?" he asked in a puzzled voice.

"No," she replied, "I just wanted to bring you this." She removed her blanket and placed it around his shoulders. Chato was shocked; he never expected anything like this.

"You may be different," she said in a gentle voice, "but you still get cold like the rest of us."

"Thanks," he blurted out, as she turned and went back to her spot and covered herself with blankets. She was different than anyone he had ever met, he told himself as he watched her close her eyes and fall asleep. The rest of the night Chato sat with his blanket around his shoulders, watching everyone sleeping around the fire. He never saw Mary wake up again but still felt as if she were watching him. Just before dawn, Zack woke and realize Chato had let him sleep in. Joining Chato, he thanked him for letting him sleep.

"See anything?" he asked as they watched the horizon starting to get light in the distance.

"Not a thing," Chato replied, "it's been quiet."

"We are lucky then," Zack told him. "I know there are more wolves out there."

"You might be right," Chato replied, as he stood and stretched.

"We better turn the horses out to graze while they can," Zack said walking towards the picket rope. Chato turned to follow him and saw Mary was awake and watching.

The Future of his People

For two more days they traveled hard all day, taking turns standing guard at night. The full moon was over, but Zack still thought they should be careful. The afternoon of the fourth day they drove their wagons into town. Chato saw the streets were full of other travelers who had gotten there ahead of them. He saw the general store, the bank, and the assay office as he drove Mary's wagon down the street.

"Where do you want to go?" he asked Mary who was sitting next to him. Mary had been sick earlier that morning, but now seem to be feeling better.

"The livery stable," she told him. "I need to see if I can sell the wagon and team for enough money to go to my aunt's farm back east." Chato drove the wagon to the livery and jumping down, turned to help Mary down. Holding her by the waist as he helped her down, Chato sensed something strong. He looked puzzled when she looked up and thanked him.

"I probably won't see you again," she said. "So I'll share this with you now. You are different from the rest of us somehow, I can feel it," she said in a gentle voice. "Maybe someday you will be famous, the president or something, I don't know. I do know you are different, and I'm not frightened of you anymore. You are special," she told him, "so take care of yourself."

Taking his hand, she thanked him again and then went into livery. As she touched his hand Chato felt the same feeling again, although not as strong as he had felt when he helped her down.

Confused by it he muttered, "Goodbye," and taking his horse walked back down the street towards the bank.

Sam Jenkins was in for the surprise of his life, and maybe his last surprise if he wasn't careful. Once inside the bank, Chato asked the teller, "Is Sam Jenkins available?"

"He is busy right now," the teller replied.

"Tell him his silver partner is here to see him," Chato sneered. Seeing the seriousness in Chato's face, the teller went quickly to the back office.

"Let him in!" he heard Sam say in a booming voice. The teller led Chato through the back and to the office. As Chato entered the office, he could see the surprise and maybe disappointment in Sam's eyes at seeing him alive.

"Chato, dear friend," Sam said, reaching out and shaking Chato's hand. "I thought you were dead. All we have been hearing about are reports of wolves killing everyone."

"I thought you might think that, so I decided to come into town and check on our money," Chato told him.

"Well, now that the mining shut down, we have both lost a lot of our money," Sam exclaimed in a sad voice. Chato smiled at him, and turning, shut the office door and pulled the shade.

In a second he had Sam by the throat. "Let me introduce you to a friend of mine," he growled as his eyes turned fiery yellow and he changed into the wolf. Sam was terrified beyond belief as he felt himself being lifted off the floor by his neck. As the wolf glared into his eyes, only inches away he fainted, going limp. Disgusted, the wolf threw him to the floor and changed back into Chato. He went to the door of the office and listen to see if anyone heard the struggle. Hearing nothing out of the ordinary, he easily lifted Sam and sat him in his big leather chair. Taking a glass half full of water from the desk, he threw it into Sam's face. As Sam came to he saw Chato standing over him.

"Now that you have met my other side," Chato told him quietly in a wicked voice. "I feel we should talk about our money and the mine." Holding Sam easily in the chair, Chato's eyes turned fiery yellow as he spoke. "I can turn wolf at any time, day or night, moon or no moon," he told Sam with a chuckle. "If you ever betray me or my kind, I will eat you alive, starting at your feet," he said smacking his lips. "I promise you, you will not enjoy it, understand?" Sam gasped for breath and nodded his head. "Good!" Chato said wickedly, "Very good! Now, lets talk about our money and the mine. My mother and Scotty will continue to mine the silver for us and I expect you to be sure they always have everything they need. I also expect you to continue to sell the silver and handle our finances. Now, on the subject of our money," Chato sneered. "When I say our, I mean my mother, Scotty, and I. You will no longer be a partner but will still be paid well enough by us so you can live comfortably." Glaring at Sam with his yellow eyes only inches away, he growled, "I expect you to transfer all but twenty five percent of your account to ours immediately. Understand?" Sam was terrified as he nodded his head.

"Good," Chato said, sitting on the desk. "I'll give you the rest of the afternoon to handle our accounts and then you can take me to supper." Standing, Chato looked down at Sam "Oh, one other thing to remember, silver bullets can't kill me, because I'm not like the others! So remember if anything happens to my family or myself I will blame you and you will die the most painful death you can imagine. Understand?" he asked in a growl.

"Yes!" Sam said in a terrified, broken voice.

"Good. I will see you later, either to enjoy eating my supper with you or to enjoy eating you for my supper." Smiling, he turned and left the office while Sam tried to regain his composure.

Before leaving the bank, Chato withdrew money from his account. He saw Sam leave the office as he left and smiled wickedly at him, waving goodbye. Once outside, he stood next to the street watching all the people pass by. Everybody had somewhere to go in a hurry. Sensing something behind him, he turned to see Mary walking towards him.

"How did your bargaining go at livery?" he asked her.

She smiled at him and said, "I would have liked to have gotten more, but I think I got enough to travel to my aunt's house. I never expected to see you again so soon," she said, smiling. "Have you found a place to stay tonight?" she asked.

"No, not yet," he replied.

"Good," she told him taking him by his arm. "I'll help you, if you help me."

Smiling at her, he chuckled, saying, "I guess you really aren't scared of me anymore, are you?"

"Sometimes, I feel like I should be," she replied. "But something inside me tells me not to be." As they walked towards the town's hotel, Chato knew that whatever was telling her not to fear him was what he could sense.

Once at the hotel, they got rooms next to each other at the top of the stairs. Taking her to her room, Chato asked her where her belongings were.

"I left them at livery," she replied, "until I could find a place to stay."

"I have to attend to my horse," he told her. "I will pick them up and bring them to you on my way back. "Oh, by the way," he said as he started down the stairs, "a banker friend of mine invited me to dinner tonight and I would really like you to join us if you would like."

"That would be nice," she replied. "When you bring me my clothes I will be ready."

Laughing at her, he went down the stairs and out of the hotel. As Mary turned and went inside her room, she thought about Vernon and her brother. It seemed like she lost them years ago now. A peace seemed to come over her, like something inside her was giving her the strength to go on. Chato was different than anyone she had ever met and despite her trying to control her fear she was still scared of him.

Once Chato took care of his horse at the livery, he picked up Mary's things and returned to the hotel. As he passed the bank, he stepped quickly inside and saw Sam working at the counter.

"Be ready in about an hour and we will go to supper," he said, looking deep into Sam's eyes and smiling. He could tell Sam was doing exactly as he had asked. "Oh, and by the way we will have a lady joining us," he told Sam as he went out the door.

Once at the hotel, he knocked on Mary's door. He heard Mary ask, "Who is it?" "It's me," he said as she opened the door.

"Please come in," she told him, stepping aside to let him bring in her things.

Setting them on the floor he said, "I'll be back in one hour and we can get something to eat."

"I'll be ready. Lately I'm always hungry." Going to his room Chato decided to rest for a few minutes before cleaning up and going to supper. Lying down on the bed, he marveled at how soft and nice the mattress felt. Closing his eyes he remembered the feeling he got when he helped Mary down from the wagon. It was strong but he still couldn't tell what it was. She puzzled him and he was starting to enjoy being around her, he thought as he soon fell asleep.

It seemed he had only closed his eyes for a second, when he heard tapping on his door. Jumping up, he opened the door to find Mary looking very nice standing before him. "Am I late?" he asked, wiping the sleep from his eyes.

"Maybe a little," she replied in a gentle voice.

"Come in and sit down while I clean up." Sitting on the only chair in the room, Mary watched him clean up and comb his hair. Knocking the dust from his hat he put it on and told Mary he was ready.

"You look nice," she told him as he opened the door for her.

"Yeah sure," he replied. "You're the one who looks nice!" As Chato walked down the stairs with her, he realized how pretty she really was. Leaving the hotel, they walked to the bank and found Sam Jenkins patiently waiting for them.

"Ma'am," he said tipping his hat.

"Take us where we can get good food," Chato said with a grin. "We're both starved."

Sam took them to the town's only restaurant, several blocks down from the bank. As they got close to the restaurant, Chato could smell all kinds of delicious food cooking inside. Once inside an elderly woman wearing an apron greeted them.

"It's good to see you tonight Sam!" she exclaimed in a quiet voice.

Sam looked quickly at Chato and then told her, "It's good to be here." She took them to a lovely table next to the large window overlooking the street. As everyone sat down, Sam introduced Chato to her.

"Sally, this is Chato, my silver mine partner and new boss."

"Hello Sally," Chato replied. "This is Mary, a friend of mine," he said nodding to Mary sitting next to him.

Wiping her hand on her apron and smiling Sally asked, "Now what can I get you folks?"

"I'm buying!" Sam exclaimed. "So don't be bashful and order exactly what you want."

Chato looked at Mary and she whispered to him she would eat

whatever he was going to have. "Okay then," he said, "bring us three thick, juicy steaks and plenty of hot coffee. Make my steak bloody rare," Chato told the waitress.

Mary looked at the waitress and said, "Make mine bloody rare also."

"Are you sure?" Chato asked. "It's almost raw."

"I'm sure," Mary said, smacking her lips.

"Make mine well-done," Sam said, grinning at Sally. As Sally went back into the kitchen, Chato looked deep into Sam's now frightened eyes. "I believe you have some documents to show me," he said in quiet voice.

"Yeah uh, sure …" Sam blurted, fumbling under his coat and removing papers from his inside coat pocket. Handing them to Chato, he watched him look at the numbers carefully. Mary could tell that Sam Jenkins was afraid of Chato. She noticed whenever Chato spoke to him, his eyes looked frightened. Chato studied the papers for a few quiet minutes and then turned to Mary sitting next to him.

"I've always had trouble with numbers and words," he said softly, looking into her eyes. "I wonder if I might bother you and ask you to help me understand these documents?"

Immediately Mary's eyes lit up; at last she could do something to repay his kindness. "Of course I will!" she exclaimed. Chato laid the documents on the table in front of her. "Let me see," she said, reading both documents. "They are receipts," she muttered. "One is your account and the other is Sam Jenkins. My …" she said in surprise, "the total quantity in your account is very large."

"How does it compare to Mr. Jenkins' account?" Chato asked, looking at Sam. He knew as he looked at Sam, he had done what he asked for, or Sam would be running for his life.

"Your total is much larger," Mary leaned over and whispered to him.

"Good!" Chato replied, gathering the papers and placing them in his pocket. "It's a pleasure doing business with you, Sam," he said, reaching out and shaking Sam's trembling hand. "I'm sure we will be in business for many long years to come."

When the steaks came, Mary was surprised at how much she enjoyed the tender, juicy meat, with blood oozing out. Halfway through her steak she realized who Chato was. He was one of the partners of the silver mine they had just fled from. No wonder she felt the way she did when he was around her! She remembered tales and legends about the wolf people and it frightened her. She knew the wolves were real! Something inside her told her not to be afraid of him. Her body had been telling her not to fear what her mind was frightened of. Chato took his time enjoying his steak, as he watched Sam wolf down his. He still had almost a third of his steak left when Sam finished his. Wiping his mouth with his napkin, Sam said quietly he had a few things he still needed to do at the bank.

"Nice meeting you ma'am," he said, smiling at Mary. Looking at Chato he asked, "Are you going to be in town long?"

"I'm not sure," Chato answered. "I'm not going back to the mine if that's what you mean. I know you will take care of business for me."

"Certainly!" Sam exclaimed. "Certainly!" as he walked to the door and left the restaurant.

As they ate their steaks in silence, Mary suddenly asked, "Why is that man so frightened of you?" in a calm voice.

Chato was surprised by her openness. Wiping his mouth with his napkin he replied, "What makes you say that?"

"You can see it in his eyes and everything he does when he is around you," Mary answered.

"Sam has no reason to fear me," Chato stated. "He helps to make sure our silver mine continues to run and I need him."

"Maybe so," she said eating another bite of steak, "but he is still very frightened of you."

Chato smiled at her. He had never met anyone who talked frankly to him the way she did. As he ate his steak, he wondered if she would say the things she did now if she knew he was wolf. Chuckling, he smiled at her and thought it probably wouldn't matter to her at all.

Once they had finished their steaks, Chato asked her if she was ready to leave.

"I'm ready, I'm so stuffed I need to take a walk in order to feel better." Leaving the restaurant, they stood on the boardwalk next to the street and breathed in the fresh night air. Mary looked up into the night sky and saw all the stars scattered across it. "No moon tonight," she said, looking at Chato.

"That's okay," Chato told her. "The night sky is just as beautiful without it. Can I take you back to your room?" he asked.

"No, I think I'll walk a bit to help digest that delicious steak."

"Would you mind if I walk with you?" he asked.

"No not at all," she said with a smile as she took his arm. Together they walked down the street, arm in arm. Strolling down the street, Chato could feel the wolf in him want to emerge. It wasn't long until they had walked through the small town and into the outskirts. The farther away from the lights they walked, the harder it was for him to resist the wolf. As Mary walked slowly by his side, she felt her body telling her she had been right all along. The feelings she got when around him were the same as what she felt inside her, and now she knew why. "Why did you leave the silver mine?" Mary asked him in a soft voice.

Stopping, he turned to her and replied, "Why do you ask?"

She could tell he was startled, and quickly took one of his hands in hers. "From those documents you let me read earlier, I saw you are a rich man as well as a partner in the mine," she said softly. "That means you must be one of the two original owners who lived on the mountain all your life."

"Yes," he replied again, confused by what he was sensing, holding her hand.

"You are one of the wolf people that legends speak of, aren't you?" she said, tenderly taking his other hand. Chato's head was spinning. Now holding both her hands, the wolf in him was sensing something strong about her. "I saw your eyes turn yellow the other night," she whispered to him.

"You saw what?" Chato blurted in surprise.

"I saw your eyes turn yellow just like my Vernon's eyes turned yellow before he turned into a wolf," she told him in a calm voice.

"Mary, do you know what you're saying?" he told her in a stern voice.

"Yes," she replied. "At first I wasn't sure, but now I can feel you have the wolf in you." She held his hands even tighter.

"How would you know what the wolf feels like?" Chato exclaimed, his eyes starting to turn yellow.

"Because, I have the wolf in my body," she told him gently. "Right here!" she pulled his hands to her and placed them on her stomach. Chato's eyes were fiery yellow and he could feel the wolf in him emerging, as she placed his open hands on her body. Almost wolf now, he realized that was what he had been sensing about her. He was more powerful than any of the others, even his mother, but couldn't tell what the feeling was until now. Mary held his hands against her and watched him turn into the wolf.

"I know you will not hurt me!" she said in a trembling voice to the snarling wolf. Suddenly the wolf was gone and Chato was again standing before her.

"You never screamed or ran away!" he muttered in shock.

"I'm one of you now. The child inside me is a wolf."

Amazed, he looked into her eyes, saying, "This child will be like me, not like the others. He will have the same powers I have!"

"Good!" she said, still holding his hands against her. "I want you to be his father and teach him how to survive, if you will have me."

"Do you know what you are saying?" he asked. "As the wolf, we will kill many of your kind. Is that what you want?"

"The wolf in my unborn child is being nurtured by my body and is nurturing me, making my body not a wolf, but not what I was before. I saw my Vernon killed because he was the wolf and I won't let my baby die the same way," she said in a pleading voice.

Admiring her bravery and beauty, he looked deep into her eyes. "Perhaps you are the one I have been looking for," Chato said, looking tenderly at her. "If you will have me, together we can be the future of my people, the people of the wolf!"